BOUND

Books by Donna Jo Napoli

Breath
The Great God Pan
Daughter of Venice
Beast
Crazy Jack
Spinners (with Richard Tchen)
Sirena
For the Love of Venice
Stones in the Water
Song of the Magdeline
Zel
The Magic Circle

BOUND

DONNA JO NAPOLI ATHENEUM BOOKS FOR YOUNG READERS
NEW YORK   LONDON   TORONTO   SYDNEY

For Michael Chen, who introduced me to the
three perfections, and for Lii Ying and Yuh Teh Chen,
who helped me try to understand them.

Atheneum Books for Young Readers • An imprint of Simon & Schuster
Children's Publishing Division • 1230 Avenue of the Americas, New York, New
York 10020 • This book is a work of fiction. Any references to historical events,
real people, or real locales are used fictitiously. Other names, characters, places,
and incidents are products of the author's imagination, and any resemblance to
actual events or locales or persons, living or dead, is entirely coincidental. •
Copyright © 2004 by Donna Jo Napoli • All rights reserved, including the right
of reproduction in whole or in part in any form. • Book design by Kristin Smith •
The text for this book is set in Hoefler Text. • Manufactured in the United
States of America • First Edition • 10 9 8 7 6 5 4 3 2 1 • Library of Congress
Cataloging-in-Publication Data • Napoli, Donna Jo, 1948– • Bound / Donna Jo
Napoli. • p.   cm. • Summary: In a novel based on Chinese Cinderella tales,
fourteen-year-old stepchild Xing Xing endures a life of neglect and servitude, as
her stepmother cruelly mutilates her own child's feet so that she alone might
marry well. • ISBN 0-689-86175-3 • 1. China—History—Ming dynasty, 1368–
1644—Juvenile fiction. [1. China—History—Ming dynasty, 1368–1644—Fiction.
2. Stepmothers—Fiction. 3. Footbinding—Fiction. 4. Sex role—Fiction.]
I. Cinderella. English. II. Title. • PZ7.N15Bo 2004 • [Fic]—dc22 • 2004000365

ACKNOWLEDGMENTS

Thanks to my family, first and foremost, for suggestions all along the way. And to Alan Berkowitz, Norian Caporale-Berkowitz, Lii Ying and Yuh Teh Chen, Shizhe Huang, Li-ching Mair, and Richard Tchen for comments on earlier versions. Thanks also to Victor Mair for allowing me to read his forthcoming article "The First Recorded Cinderella Story" and to Haili Kong for answering some of my questions about Ming China. A special thanks to Mary Reindorp and her second-period sixth-grade language arts class at Strath Haven Middle School in fall 2003. And a most fundamental thanks goes to Brenda Bowen, Jordan Brown, and Cindy Nixon. Any errors that remain are my own.

Note to reader: The name of the main character, Xing Xing, is pronounced "Shing Shing."

1 Xing Xing squatted by the water, silent and unmoving. Her stillness was a prayer.

It was answered: The sun glinted red. Only an instant and it was over, but there could be no doubt; her eyes had not played tricks: A white fish with red fins and golden eyes zipped past and under a lotus leaf. She laughed in delight.

"Lazy One, bring the firewood," came the distant call.

In the past year "Lazy One" had practically become Xing Xing's household name. She imagined her father's wife holding one hand above her eyes against the sun that was so bright today, it had already burned off the morning fog. She imagined her frowning in impatience, then ducking back into the shadows of the cave. The girl picked up the armful of wood she'd gathered and rushed back along the path. Her hair was tied in two hanging knots that thumped on her shoulders as she ran. *Hurry,* they drummed, *hurry hurry*. The cold dirt licked at her feet. *Hurry hurry*.

But she was wrong. Stepmother had not gone inside. The woman shivered in the chill of spring, arms crossed over her chest. "Get inside, Lazy One." She yanked one of Xing Xing's hair knots as the girl raced past through the open door.

The air of the main cavern had changed already. While the roof was so thick that the temperature hardly varied from summer to winter, the quality of the air could change drastically. Right now it had grown clammy. Xing Xing knelt and fed tinder to the coals of the dying fire, then sticks, then the wood she'd just brought in. The door squeaked shut behind her. Stepmother didn't oil the hinges on purpose because the noise scared away demons. Xing Xing got to her feet and turned around to find Stepmother standing right there, her hands on her hips, her muscled arms cocked like wings.

"Wood doesn't grow from springs," said Stepmother.

Xing Xing knew this was Stepmother's way of asking why she'd come from the direction of the pond rather than the woods. She'd seen the beautiful pool fish twice now—yesterday afternoon and again this morning. It was her secret. Stubbornness entered her. She looked in Stepmother's eyes without blinking.

"But water does." Stepmother hobbled over and picked up the water bucket and carrying pole. She hobbled back and put one in each of Xing Xing's hands. "Are you waiting for grass to grow under your feet?"

Xing Xing ran out the door again, leaving it open. She rushed through the buzz of the bees they kept in the hive on the side of their cave. *Rush rush, buzz buzz.*

"My daughter will wake soon," called Stepmother after her. "And hunger hurts."

Xing Xing returned to the pond, only too happily. She filled the bucket, then walked around the edge, looking. The thought of Stepmother's daughter waking and complaining of hunger quickened her pace. It wasn't that her half sister would be truly hungry, not like the old beggar men who wandered the village, hands outstretched, and slept at night under the raised floor of the public pavilion. Rather, her half sister's stomach would simply have emptied of the meal she ate last night. But she felt so poorly these days that Xing Xing didn't want to allow even that small amount of extra discomfort. Besides, her complaints could result in a smack on the head for Xing Xing.

Xing Xing was practically running now.

The fish didn't show itself.

Well, of course not. Secrets could never be rushed. They had to come of their own accord, on their own schedule. That way, when they came, they offered themselves as a gift.

Xing Xing leaned over the water, extending her right cheek till she could feel the wetness that hovered in the air close to the pond's surface. "Later," she sang. Then she stood and turned in a circle, lifting her chin so both her cheeks could brush the dry air. This was her way of caressing the spirit of her mother so that she could feel close by. She balanced the bucket on one end of the pole and put the other end over her shoulder, then walked home without spilling a drop.

2 Wei Ping slept sideways across the bed with her legs dangling over the edge. Her mother, Stepmother, had rolled the rock from the high hole that served as a window, so sunbeams played on her chest. She opened her eyes, rose to sitting, and stretched one thin leg. Her face grimaced with pain as she rubbed behind that knee. She did the same to the other leg. A tear escaped and ran down her cheek. Her lips tightened into a wide line. She looked at the gaily-colored bandages around her feet, and the very corners of her mouth rose in satisfaction.

Xing Xing could tell Wei Ping was admiring herself—an immodest act that one should avoid both practicing and witnessing in others. Xing Xing looked down at her own feet, but too late, for Wei Ping happened to glance at her first.

"No one cares about your feet," hissed Wei Ping. She grabbed one of the stools waiting by the bedstead and searched around for the other. It had somehow tumbled out of reach. "Get me that stool, Lazy One."

Xing Xing pushed the stool to her half sister.

Wei Ping knelt with one knee on each stool and took a loud, deep breath. Then she threw her weight on one knee and moved the other stool forward with her hands. She threw her weight on the other knee and moved the second stool forward with her hands. In this manner, she worked her way over to the *kang*, never putting weight on her feet. The *kang* was the most-used piece of furniture in their home—where one could eat and talk and sew and even nap. It was adjacent to the stove, with a fire passage inside its stone slabs. Heat from the cooking fire passed under it, then out through the chimney in the roof of the cave. As Wei Ping passed Xing Xing, she spat on her toes. "No one will find you a husband."

Xing Xing knew words spoken in pain could be far crueler than the speaker really intended. Still, she had to bite the insides of her cheeks to hold in a gasp. For what Wei Ping said was true enough to cut deep.

Xing Xing's mother had died when Xing Xing was seven years old. She and Stepmother had lived side by side in the cave as the two wives of the master potter Wu, who had himself died a year ago, when Xing Xing was but thirteen. With no father or mother, there was no one to arrange a marriage for Xing Xing.

Wei Ping was only a year older than Xing Xing, but Stepmother had already begun preparations for finding her a husband. Indeed, she'd started within a month of Wu's death. Wei Ping had a face that was neither plain nor pretty, but she was slender as a reed, exactly as men preferred their wives. If she'd had her feet bound at the age of six, when Stepmother had first proposed it to Wu, her feet would be small enough to fit in a man's hand like a golden lotus blossom, and she'd already undoubtedly be betrothed. But though both of Wu's wives had tiny bound feet, the potter didn't want his daughters' feet bound. He had grown up way down south, where not so many women bound their feet, and he didn't like the custom. Besides, he had enjoyed the assistance of his daughters in his shop—and that work required them to have full use of their feet.

Stepmother had argued that Wu could hire labor for the shop or buy a slave girl to help out. After all, they hired labor to help in the household chores. The potter wouldn't hear of it; if strangers saw him at work, they might sell the secrets of his special ways to other potters.

Stepmother had argued that, despite her small size, Xing Xing was exceptionally strong while Wei Ping was delicate; Xing Xing could do the work of both girls. But the potter said that exalting the daughter Wei Ping over the daughter Xing Xing would go precisely contrary to his dead wife's wishes. Anyway, out here in the country, foot binding generally didn't start till a girl reached puberty, unlike in the city, where it started sometimes even before the child turned six.

Stepmother lamented. She'd wake her husband in the morning with her hand in front of his face, fingers spread to the length of Wei Ping's feet, screeching about *zhang*—growth—and quoting sayings from the first teacher, Kong Fu Zi—Master Kong—about doing the right thing at the right moment. Still, Wu insisted that Stepmother wait.

Once he was dead, though, the woman lost no time. Wei Ping's feet were already as long as the full spread of Stepmother's fingers, much longer than Xing Xing's feet, but the woman swore that with the proper binding, they could shrink.

Xing Xing drained the pot of boiling water chestnuts. Then she poured them onto the mat tray and shook the tray gently, so they'd roll around and cool off faster.

Wei Ping moaned from the *kang*.

"Lazy One," said Stepmother, "my daughter is hungry."

Xing Xing knew the moan was because Wei Ping's feet hurt, but no one was allowed to talk about that. Besides, Xing Xing avoided saying anything to Stepmother unless it was absolutely necessary. She peeled the steaming nuts as fast as she could, blowing on her fingers the whole while.

3 Stepmother sat on the stone bench outside the cave entrance sewing. She was making a fine dress for Wei Ping.

Xing Xing passed behind her, quiet as a plumed egret.

"Flat feet make noise no matter what," said Stepmother. "Even stunted ones like yours." She pulled a strip of cloth out of a purse tied to her sleeve and held it out to Xing Xing. "My daughter needs meat for supper."

Xing Xing's mouth twisted in worry; she was a poor hunter of land creatures. The range of things Stepmother expected her to do kept growing. This was the third time within a month that she'd handed Xing Xing that hunting cloth.

But Wei Ping really did need meat. When Xing Xing washed her half sister's foot bandages, she had to scrub hard to get the bloodstains out. And lately

Wei Ping's feet oozed a foul-smelling yellow liquid that seemed to drain away her energy. Meat brought energy, and Xing Xing knew a good hunter.

So the girl tied the cloth around her waist and ran down the hill to the edge of the village, where Tang, the master painter, lived, calling out softly, "See me, Mother? I'm going to visit Master Tang."

The master sat outside in his courtyard under the tangled branches of a willow, smoothing the hairs on his paintbrushes. The yellow finches in the cage that swung above his head twittered to the sounds of the large arrow bamboo leaves rustling in the breeze. The orchid pots Xing Xing's own father had made stood grouped together in one corner. Surrounding them were ink green indigo plants. She bowed deeply, then sat on her heels beside the old man.

"Ah, the hunting cloth serves as your belt, Pretty Child," said Master Tang. "My boy is already in the woods, alas. He will bring home only as much as our household needs."

Xing Xing kept her breath steady in her disappointment. She had, in fact, guessed the situation, since the slave boy was nowhere in sight. Master Tang's boy typically stayed by the old man's side if he was home.

"But I am in need of some assistance at the moment. If an hour's labor interests you, I could offer you a sack of polliwogs as your payment."

Polliwogs swirled in profusion in the rushes at the sides of the slow river that hugged the bottom of the hill near Xing Xing's cave. Master Tang had a taste for frogs, so every spring he had his slave boy fill outdoor tubs with polliwogs. That way, when they matured, he could eat frogs at the slightest whim, with no wait. The last thing Xing Xing wanted was polliwogs. Watching frogs made her laugh; she couldn't bear to eat them.

Master Tang had always been good to her, however. He and Father had been friends. And until just a year ago he had been one of her teachers. Before potter Wu moved to this area, no one had heard of an ordinary person getting an education. None of the boys around here was educated, much less the girls. But Wu had his own ways. Some people hadn't liked him because of that. They said he gave himself airs— he acted as though he thought he was better than they were, when he was nothing but a simple potter. Master Tang wasn't like that; Master Tang had been Father's true friend.

"Thank you for the kindness, Venerable Elder." Xing Xing bowed her head.

"Come."

Master Tang led Xing Xing inside, to the room where he painted. She knew her task would be to copy a poem onto the master's latest painting. She was good at calligraphy; Master Tang told her she was very good.

Father used to stand over Xing Xing and Wei Ping for hours as they worked on calligraphy. He spoke of the three incomparables—the three perfections: painting, poetry, calligraphy. Master Tang instructed the girls in painting, his wife instructed them in poetry, but Father himself instructed them in calligraphy. Perhaps that was why Xing Xing excelled in the third perfection. When Father was alive, she had worked hard for his approval, much harder than Wei Ping ever had.

After Father died, Wei Ping stopped all her lessons. She'd never wanted those lessons in the first place, and now the pain in her feet broke her concentration, and she couldn't leave the cave anyway. Stepmother was relieved; an educated girl would be harder to marry off. That Xing Xing should continue her lessons alone was out of the question.

Nevertheless, each day when Xing Xing visited Father's grave to say hello and apologize again for no

having been at his side when he died, she practiced calligraphy in the dry dirt over the point where she imagined his stomach to be. After all, wisdom resided in the stomach, and she wanted Father's wisdom to refine her motions; she wanted his guidance and approval even more these days than she had when he was alive. Her art had not deteriorated in the period since his death.

Xing Xing sat on the floor now and looked carefully at Master Tang's new painting. In the foreground was a home on a cliff with a pear tree in blossom; in the background, a bay cradled by mountains. This was a scene from the long, long coastline that Xing Xing had never seen. Master Tang had once lived in a coastal town near where the Yangzi River emptied into the huge ocean. He painted from memory.

Xing Xing unlocked the closet where Master Tang kept all the supplies. She took out, first of all, the inlaid box that held the top-quality inkstone, then the ink, then, for visual harmony, the same brush that Master Tang had used to paint this picture. There was an old pear tree in Master Tang's courtyard, right near the cassias. She went to stand by it and opened her nostrils, letting the fragrance of the flowers float inside her, before she took the cap off the paintbrush.

For the next hour Xing Xing dipped that finest

brush in the blackest ink mixed on that most beautiful inkstone, and with loving care, she copied the poem on Master Tang's painting. She wrote between the mountains and the bellied sails of a boat at sea. They were not words in the sky or in the sea—ridiculous thought—they were words simply in space. If a painting called for words, as most did, there was always a space that held those words perfectly. Father had taught her that, for she had sometimes added words to the bowls or vases he made.

She sang the poem to herself as she worked. It was brief, but every poem was worthy of extreme attention, and this one pleased her very much:

> *Pear blossoms fall soft white*
> *Recalling snow past beyond sight*
> *Revealing warmth ahead in sun's light*

The poem, Xing Xing knew, came from the mouth of Master Tang's only remaining wife, Mei Zi, the wife who had instructed both Xing Xing and Wei Ping in poetry and whose hands were too twisted with arthritis now to be entrusted with a painting. The girl hoped that the warmth ahead in summer sun would hurry and ease the old woman's suffering.

4 Xing Xing's first thought was to free the polliwogs Master Tang had given her into the spring-fed pool near her home, but then she thought of the beautiful fish in that pool. A mature frog could eat a fish that size.

She changed directions and went instead to the river rushes, where she opened the small sack and watched the polliwogs gleefully escape. They had four legs already, but their tails still remained—frog, but not yet fully frog.

Then she headed for the woods. If she was lucky, she'd pass Master Tang's slave boy and beg him to catch her at least a few quails. The boy was clearly sweet on her. He gaped whenever she passed. Xing Xing did nothing to encourage his attentions. Her life was far too busy with obeying Stepmother and caring for Father's spirit to think about such things yet. Whenever the boy did her a favor, she always made sure she did him a favor in return, so as never to be beholden to him. But she didn't expect to be lucky enough to pass him in the woods now. One of the reasons the boy was such a good hunter was that he could move so silently and swiftly that the animals didn't realize he was near. It wasn't likely that Xing Xing would be able to detect him.

She walked quietly herself, but in order to be that quiet, she had to move very slowly.

Faint squeals came from somewhere close off to the right. Xing Xing held her breath and followed the sounds.

In a clearing at the foot of a large pine was a raccoon kit. Another came squealing behind it. And a third scrabbled out from under a scrub bush.

Xing Xing looked around quickly. Kits this young would undoubtedly still be under the care of a mother, and mother raccoons were fierce. She stooped and picked up a rock, more for protection than anything else. No sensible hunter would kill a mother before her young could survive on their own.

The mother didn't come, however. And soon enough Xing Xing realized things were amiss. The kits stumbled around, but not in the fashion of babes just learning to walk. Rather, they walked fine, but they tripped over rocks and knocked into the trunk of the pine. The girl came closer, checking over her shoulder for the mother.

The kits stopped, their noses twitching. They'd caught her scent. Now they ran in panic in three directions, falling and slamming into things as they went. Why, they were blind!

The poor things. They'd never survive on their own. And that's why the mother was nowhere around, of course. She must have realized something was wrong and simply left them to their fate.

Xing Xing stopped moving.

Within minutes, the kits squealed again. After all, if the strange scent had been a mortal threat, it would have attacked by now. They grouped together, linked by sound and scent.

If she abandoned them, as the mother had done, they'd be dead by evening. Sooner, probably. They were meat to any passing carnivore no matter what Xing Xing did.

Wei Ping needed meat.

Xing Xing untied the hunting cloth from around her waist. She put the rock in it and slung it hard at a kit. The little thing didn't even let out a cry. But the thump of the rock scared the other two. They screamed and ran in circles.

Xing Xing wiped at her nose, which always ran when she was sad. It was unnatural to kill babies, but it made no sense not to kill these. In fact, a swift death with a stone was more humane then letting them be ripped limb from limb by a wolf. She took the rock and slung it hard at another kit. It missed the mark. She fetched it before she lost her resolve and slung it again. The kit fell dead.

Xing Xing picked up a dead kit in each hand. Then she sank to her knees, her arms as limp by her sides as the small bodies in her hands. "Mother," she called out. "Stay with me, Mother."

The spirit of her mother brushed her cheeks. The girl closed her eyes and let the spirit brush her eyelids, her ears, her temples, her lips.

Now the spirit brushed the back of her right hand. It took a nip. Ouch.

Xing Xing opened her eyes. The third kit had gone from testing her hand to nosing his dead brother. If she didn't stop him fast, he'd turn cannibal.

Xing Xing let herself fall onto the live kit, so that he was caught under her pelvis. She quickly closed her skirts around him, trapping him there with one hand, while she gathered up the hunting cloth and the two dead kits with the other.

5 Stepmother's eyebrows, which always arched high in the thinnest of pencil lines, arched even higher at the sight of the dead kits. But when she realized the live kit was blind, she nodded in silent accord. She opened an old birdcage on the floor, and Xing Xing guided the kit into it.

"We'll feed him, and when he's big and plump, we'll eat hearty," said Stepmother.

"No, no. It's better that he should be a pet," said Wei Ping. "I can play with him."

"Wild creatures make poor pets," said Stepmother, but she spoke hesitantly. Xing Xing watched the conflict in her face. Pain rendered her daughter practically a prisoner these days; indeed, the girl was still sitting on the *kang,* where she'd been since she woke. She needed amusement—anyone could hear that in the strain of her voice. Stepmother got the knife and set to cleaning the two dead raccoon kits.

Without being told, Xing Xing went outside for fresh water, this time taking only the medium-size pail. She made a quick diversion to Father's grave first, so that she could tell his spirit about the raccoon kits—about how hard it was to kill them and how small the remaining one was, how very dear. As she talked, she tenderly brushed away leaves that had fallen on the grave and creepers that were starting to grow across it. Sparrows twittered, magpies raucously clamored, thrushes warbled. The birds let her know that Father understood.

She scooted back to the path and hurried down to the pool. She dipped the pail in the water and, oh, what on earth had happened? She stared. The beautiful fish swam in the pail. Xing Xing laughed. "You're so lovely," she said. "White as a peony." The peony was Xing Xing's favorite flower, because it had been Mother's favorite flower.

She splashed a little water on the dirt at her feet and picked up a stick to draw with. She wrote her own poem:

> *Fins like red clouds at sunset*
> *Eyes like gold tears of joy, sparkling wet*
> *White fish in cold water, happily met*

Then she tipped the pail till it emptied, for who could catch such loveliness? But when she refilled the pail, the fish swam into it again. She emptied it and refilled. Once more the fish swam into the pail.

It would be unwise to ignore such insistence. So Xing Xing carried home the pail. But before she entered the cave, she hid the pail behind a boulder and went straight into the back of the cave to the small room with a ceiling so low that you had to crawl within it. That's where Stepmother stored the few bowls and pots remaining from Father's working days. Every now and then she sold one. That was their sole source of income. Stepmother said that Wei Ping would be married before the storeroom was empty, though, so they had no cause for fear. Wei Ping's husband would take care of all of them. And if by some mistake of chance the storeroom emptied prematurely, there were other solutions.

Xing Xing fervently hoped a husband would come for her half sister soon, for she knew of the most likely other solution: Stepmother would sell her, and with the money, she could buy a younger girl to help around the cave and still have enough left over to wait for a husband for Wei Ping. Though Xing Xing's life had been reduced to hardly more than that of a slave girl since Father's death, she feared being sold. She was clearly a young woman, and at her age slavery could mean the very worst fate for a female.

So Xing Xing moved within the black air of the storeroom with the utmost care. It would never do to break a bowl. Her blood banged in her temples. She shouldn't be taking such a risk for a fish. Yet memory urged her on. Her fingers played on every object till she found exactly the bowl she sought, the one with the scalloped edges.

She backed out of the storeroom, clutching the bowl to her chest. When she emerged, Stepmother was there, waiting.

"What could this mean?" she asked in anger. "Am I to change your name from 'Lazy One' to 'Wicked One'?"

Xing Xing bowed. "Amusement for my sister," she said. She ran past Stepmother and brought back the pail. Then she filled the bowl with water and scooped the fish from the pail into the bowl.

"What nonsense is this?" asked Stepmother.

"Let me see," called Wei Ping.

Xing Xing carried over the bowl and set it on the *kang* beside her half sister.

Sunlight danced on the bowl's enamel, where brilliant yellows and greens and reds played out the legendary story of the carp at Dragon Gate. The yellow carp fight their way upstream in spring. Some of them try to leap Dragon Gate. According to common belief, a tremendous storm follows this fight and sets afire the tails of those bravest fish that succeed, turning them into dragons. The outside of the bowl pictured a frenzy of jumping fish; the inside, the blaze of a single dragon. And in the very center of the inside was one word, which Xing Xing herself had written: *li*. Saying that syllable with the tone of the voice dipping and then rising in pitch, it meant "carp"; saying that same syllable with the tone of the voice falling from a high to a low pitch, it meant "advantage." The spoken word was a pun about the story illustrated on the bowl, and Xing Xing had thought of it herself, much to the delight of Father, who was a master of puns.

"Look at the fins on this fish," said Wei Ping. "They're red already. This fish wants to become a dragon." She smiled.

Xing Xing could hardly remember the last time Wei Ping had smiled.

"Struggle has its rewards," said Stepmother. And she looked at Xing Xing with approval.

Xing Xing could not remember Stepmother ever having looked at her with approval. Inside her head she thanked the lovely fish.

6 Xing Xing sat in the dark under the stars. Father used to say this habit cleansed the mind and formed a base for the understanding of things. She was in need of understanding.

Stepmother's look this afternoon had unnerved her. She wanted to see that look again. It had been a long time since Xing Xing had felt anyone cared for her.

She missed that terribly, for her parents had been devoted to her, despite the fact that she was born a girl. Her mother used to say that Xing Xing was precious and dazzling, her "Sparkling One." That's why she had named her Xing Xing, meaning "stars." And her father had taken great pride in her cleverness.

When Xing Xing's mother lay dying of the illness that twisted her insides and made her cough blood, she said that her *hun,* her spirit, would always protect Xing Xing. And she had asked her daughter for one promise, one promise only: that Xing Xing would take care of her father's needs better than anyone else for the rest of his life and that she would be the one to eventually listen to her father's final words.

Stepmother heard the request and sucked in her breath loudly in disapproval. Such bald talk of feelings between parent and child was not traditional. The whole thing was shameful, scandalous.

Father heard as well, but he didn't care one bit about scandal. He insisted that the deathbed wish be respected. From that point on, Xing Xing alone served Father his meals and washed his hair and feet and sang to him in moments of sadness.

This was the start of Stepmother's distaste for Xing Xing—at least, so far as the girl could tell. With each passing year, Stepmother's jealousy of her grew until, in the end, the woman hardly looked at her without curling her lip. Xing Xing was never certain why Mother had made her deathbed wish. Surely she had to know that it would gall Stepmother to see Xing Xing taking on these wifely duties. Maybe Mother had feared that after she was no longer around to protect her daughter, Xing Xing would become as unimportant as she actually did become after Father died—especially if Stepmother had gone on to have a son. Xing Xing could never know.

But at least one very good thing for Stepmother came out of the strengthened bond between Father and Xing Xing: She grew closer to her own daughter. She had not treasured Wei Ping before. Indeed, the girl used to be called "First Child," nothing more. Stepmother was fond of repeating the popular saying "Better one deformed son than many daughters wise as Buddha." In both cities and villages, newborn girls were often thrown away, their bodies eaten by dogs and rats. Xing Xing's mother had been fragile and vulnerable, whereas Stepmother was always strong and large. So no one had expected Xing Xing's mother to be a good breeder—no one was surprised or disappointed that she had only one child, and a girl, at that—but everyone had expected Stepmother to be an exceptional breeder. The woman simply assumed she'd have son after son. It was fortunate that Stepmother had not thrown away her daughter like others had done, for though she worshipped the White-Robed Guan Yin all her married life, the goddess brought her no son. In fact, no other children at all. When Xing Xing's mother died and left her in charge of Father, Stepmother turned to her daughter for comfort and finally gave her a real name.

Xing Xing understood all of that. And she was sincerely happy to see Wei Ping cherished at last.

But, oh, how she wanted to be cherished too, cherished like she used to be.

And how she wanted to laugh with someone. Father used to tell jokes. She laughed with him all the time. But Stepmother had no sense of humor, nor did Wei Ping.

Still, she should be grateful. After all, Father was unfortunate enough to be the last of his family, and Mother's family would never take in a girl relative. Xing Xing was lucky Stepmother had not turned her out. Maybe with time, Xing Xing's obedience would impress her and the woman would come to care a little for her stepdaughter.

From a jujube tree nearby came the sound of scratching. The kit was clawing noisily at the spokes of the birdcage that kept it both safe and imprisoned. When Wei Ping had gone to bed, Xing Xing had hung the cage there on the chance that the raccoon, a naturally nocturnal animal, would recognize night even in his blindness and make so much noise inside that he'd wake everyone up. Her mouth opened softly in interest at his activity now. The kit couldn't be hungry, for Wei Ping had fed him continually whenever he woke all afternoon. The little creature turned out to be a glutton for boiled soybeans.

Xing Xing fingered the hole that the kit had made in her skirt as she'd carried it home today. What terrible thing could a person do in one life to make it come back in the next as a blind raccoon kit?

She shivered, alone on the rock ledge, in the black.

But then she dipped a hand in the bowl of cool water beside her. The beautiful fish sucked at her fingertips. She knew it would. Carp are funny like that. And it wasn't hunger that made the carp do that either, for Wei Ping had also fed the fish all afternoon—bits of dried apple and wine-saturated dates. What wonderful thing could a person do in one life to make it come back in the next as a marvelous white fish with red fins destined to become a dragon?

She waved her wet fingers in the air, painting on the night. Master Tang always said painting that didn't ask for calligraphy was silent poetry, expressing feelings that couldn't be put into words. Xing Xing filled the sky with her fluttering fingers.

7 The next month in the cave passed in a new balance, almost a harmony. Both the raccoon and the fish grew so steadily that Stepmother named the first Zhang Yi—Growth One—and the second Zhang Er. She threatened continually to kill them for a feast, but it was said in teasing, for her eyes betrayed her satisfaction at Wei Ping's vigorous objections—finally the girl was taking an interest in something again. Xing Xing never entered the fray, but stood behind her half sister in silent support. Both girls had grown terribly fond of the kit and the fish.

In their union against Stepmother's threats the girls found a comradeship they'd never known before. Wei Ping was no longer jealous of Xing Xing for being loved by Father, given that now she was the only loved one in the cave. And Xing Xing couldn't harbor jealousy toward Wei Ping because her foot pain was so pitiable, though Stepmother still allowed no one to talk about that.

Stepmother spent a lot of time away from home these days, renewing friendships with women she hadn't visited for years. During Father's lifetime her friends had shunned her: They accused her of aspiring to a higher social class. Now she made every effort to show them that she was still the same woman she used to be and that her daughter, Wei Ping, would make a suitable wife for a man of the social class a potter's daughter belonged to rightfully. She painted her face red and white, penciled in her eyebrows, anointed her hair with pork fat to make it stand in peaks on the back of her neck, shook bells out the window to scare demons away from the home in her absence, and headed to the village. Xing Xing watched her slow progress, her round body formless within the loose pants and long sackcloth of mourning that came well below her knees. Her gait was unsteady as she hobbled on the heels of those small feet.

Once as the girls watched Stepmother leave, Wei Ping said, "See the swing of her hips, see how sexy it is. I'll walk like that soon."

But that gait tired Stepmother out, and sometimes she came home carried on the back of a peasant man whom she'd reward with a slip of paper money.

Twice she had brought home old women who made a profession of being go-betweens for marriage—they found husbands for young girls. But both had taken one look at Wei Ping's long feet and declared her not marriageable to a man of their social class, so they'd been dismissed. Stepmother continued her visits to friends, hoping she'd come across a more amenable go-between in the process.

The half sisters therefore had long hours alone together. In that time Xing Xing scrubbed the stone wall behind the stove till it shone. She swept the floor. She straightened all the bowls and jars on the tables against the far wall. She cleaned the picture over Wei Ping's bed that had the characters saying, *Fine beauty and great wealth,* meant to invite luck. She gathered firewood. She emptied the chamber pot onto the dung heap behind the cave. She did all the chores she'd always done. But still there was time, and since Wei Ping was alone, Xing Xing stayed at home rather than going to tend to Father's grave. The half sisters soon came to confide in each other.

"Maybe you should sleep with your feet raised on a pillow," whispered Xing Xing as the girls sat on the *kang* one morning feeding the beautiful fish from their hands, while Stepmother was outside examining the jujube trees, which were now thick with green dates. "When my feet hurt, it helps to raise them. Instead, you hang yours over the bed, which seems the very worst thing to do."

"No, no," said Wei Ping. "I hang my legs over the bed so that the pressure of the bedstead behind my knees will dull the pain. You have no idea how bad it is." She clenched her teeth, and saliva made them shine like pearls. She clutched the calves of her legs, stretched out on the warm *kang*. "But I think it's working. They look smaller, don't they?"

"Yes, smaller." Xing Xing said this without conviction, however, for the bandages on her half sister's feet were large and unrevealing. They also were stinking and seeping—it was time for their periodic soaking in hot water and cleaning in the river. To hide the doubt in her eyes, Xing Xing looked down into the bowl on her lap. The beautiful fish had grown so much, it could barely turn around. She'd have to crawl into the storeroom and find something bigger—a pot for holding large plants, perhaps.

"And my nose," said Wei Ping, lifting her chin and turning her head so Xing Xing could see a full profile. "My nose is small, don't you think?"

"Very small," said Xing Xing. "And you are as slender as a man's dream."

"I am, aren't I? Even wearing our loose dresses, anyone can tell I have a fine form. I'm going to get married. I'm going to have sons." Wei Ping's eyes glistened. "So it's worth it." She gently petted the tummy of the sleeping raccoon that lay on her upper legs, stretched from her crotch to her knees, on its back, all four legs in the air. Since the kit had grown to full size, its position seemed that much more comical. Its mouth hung open in sleep, and its strong, pointed teeth formed a satisfied smile. Wei Ping and Xing Xing both smiled too. "Yes, it's worth it," said Wei Ping again with quiet determination.

"What's worth it?" said Stepmother, coming into the coolness of the cave.

"Are the jujube trees productive this year?" asked Wei Ping, steadfastly ignoring her mother's question.

"Very." She handed a hard green nugget to Wei Ping.

"But why did you pick one so soon?" asked Wei Ping. "They don't taste good till they turn red."

"I'm going to sell them," said Stepmother.

Wei Ping's forehead pinched in alarm. "We never sell our dates. Are we already desperate? Do you think I won't find a husband before Father's pottery runs out?"

"Of course you'll find a husband."

"No. You're afraid I won't." Wei Ping's voice rose to a thin shiver. "You could marry again, Mother. You're still attractive, and your feet are so small." Her words came with a frenzied speed. "And since Father has no other family left, your second husband would have to allow us to accompany you into the new marriage. Then we'd have more time for my feet to grow small—more time to find a husband for me."

"Hush!" Stepmother looked stricken. "How can you talk to your mother like that? Your father, even with all his crazy ideas, wouldn't have stood such insubordination. Hush!"

"Please, Mother." Wei Ping's voice got very quiet. The hysteria was gone now. "Marry again," she breathed.

"Widows of decent families do not remarry. You know that. It is a small matter to starve to death but a large matter to lose one's virtue."

"I don't want to starve to death," said Wei Ping.

"And you won't," said Stepmother. "You'll never know that kind of hunger. Nor will I lose my virtue." She twisted her neck, looking this way and that in worry. "I would never abandon the Wu family ghosts," she said loudly.

"Then what will we do?"

"That's what I've come to tell you. You will have a husband soon. The dates will ensure that." Stepmother sat down on the *kang* between the girls. "You know the benefits of red dates, of course."

"They invigorate one's spleen and benefit the kidneys," said Wei Ping.

"Yes, and that's when they are ripe. Think how much more beneficial they must be when green. All that goodness is concentrated in the bitterness, before the sugars of maturity."

"How do you know that?" asked Wei Ping.

"The spirit of my mother told me."

Xing Xing touched Stepmother's wrist involuntarily in awe. The woman recoiled. Xing Xing blinked her apology. Mother spirits never lie. And Stepmother's mother had understood much about medicine. Xing Xing looked with new appreciation at the green date in Wei Ping's hand. The tiny fruits on their jujube trees were as valuable as agates.

Stepmother stood up. "Xing Xing will pick them and sell them to a *jiang hu lang zhong,* a barefoot wandering doctor, who will use them to cure all kinds of illness. I heard last night that there is one visiting the village beyond ours, down the river valley."

"And how will that help get me a husband?" asked Wei Ping.

"Xing Xing will tell the *lang zhong* to let all his healed patients know that you were the source of their recovery, that you are the one who understands the virtues of plants. Every man values a woman with such gifts. He'll advertise you over the whole province. Word-of-mouth propaganda is the most useful."

"But I know nothing of plants," said Wei Ping.

"What flowed from my mother to me should naturally flow to you."

"It doesn't seem to have done so," said Wei Ping.

"It will, soon enough. Besides, once you're married, will it matter?" Stepmother didn't wait for an answer. She pulled the large basket from the corner. "Time for work, Lazy One."

Xing Xing put the bowl holding the fish on the *kang,* grateful for the opportunity to bow her head so Stepmother couldn't see the shock on her face at what she'd just said: "will it matter?" Stepmother had never before expressed explicitly such crass acceptance of deceit. Was Wei Ping also hiding her face?

As Xing Xing leaned over the bowl she looked

sideways at the sleeping raccoon. Whenever it woke, it was immediately hungry. And if she wasn't there to keep guard, its sense of smell could lead it to the beautiful fish. Just at that moment, as though the raccoon was responding to Xing Xing's thoughts, the skin above his nose wrinkled and he sniffed without waking. So she set the bowl inside the basket and carried it outside with her to the jujube trees, singing little comfort songs to the beautiful fish as she walked.

8 Xing Xing sat high in a jujube tree and stuck her fingers in her mouth to soothe them. She'd gathered the dates last autumn, but the job had been much easier then. She'd simply strung nets under the trees and beaten the branches with a stick. The ripe fruit dropped easily. But these green fruits had to be wrested individually from their stems. Her fingers were sore already, and she was only on the second tree of five.

It was hard to find a comfortable perch in the thorny branches. Last year Xing Xing's body had still been childlike. Now her sensitive chest and soft thighs kept getting jabbed. This was a more unpleasant task than she'd expected.

A scream sheared the air. It was like none she'd ever heard before, and it came from the cave. In her haste to get down, she fell from the tree, opening a wide gash on her forearm.

The air was filled with multiple screaming voices

now—Wei Ping and Stepmother together, as well as inhuman screams that Xing Xing realized must be coming from the raccoon. She ran as fast as she could, straight into the cave, and slipped in blood slime. At first she thought it was the blood that dripped from her own elbow, but then she saw brains and lungs and intestine and fur—all that remained of the blind raccoon kit. The stick he'd been bashed to death with lay in the midst, bits of innards clinging to it. Stepmother's blood-spattered face looked crazed as she ripped at the shredded bandages on Wei Ping's left foot. The girl had both hands in her hair and howled at the ceiling, throwing herself around.

"Hold her tight," shouted Stepmother to Xing Xing.

Xing Xing grabbed Wei Ping from behind and looked over her half sister's shoulder in horror as the bandages came away. The unnaturally arched foot that Xing Xing had seen before was now missing the two biggest toes.

"Devil raccoon," spat Stepmother. "Teeth like knives. At least he died in pieces, so his spirit will never be whole. Go for fresh water, Lazy One. Run."

Xing Xing grabbed the bucket and pole and practically flew down the hill to the pool. She was back, panting, faster than she'd ever moved before.

Stepmother washed Wei Ping's feet—the mutilated

one and the whole one—rubbing off the dead skin and kneading them more fully into the desired shape. With her thumbs, she worked in pulverized alum. "My baby," she murmured as she pressed, "my sweet baby." There was no blood from the holes where exposed bone showed. Xing Xing stared at the ragged bone ends.

"You'll be fine," said Stepmother. "You'll be fine." Her voice changed the second time she said those words. It sounded weak and strangely without emotion. "We have to hurry and bandage your feet before your blood has a chance to circulate there again," she said. "If we dawdle, you will bleed badly and the pain will be more terrible than you've ever dreamed. It will be savage. You'll wish you were dead."

Why was Stepmother saying such things? Xing Xing wanted to put her hands over Wei Ping's ears.

Wei Ping said nothing. She merely wept softly, her head heavy on her own chest. She breathed with difficulty.

"Your left foot will be smaller than your right now," said Stepmother.

Wei Ping still said nothing.

"So if you want me to act properly, I must do it fast," said Stepmother. "Remember the old saying: 'The eagle swoops down when the hare stirs.' You are not the first girl in China to lose a toe on a bound foot. Even without raccoon devils, it happens. And smart girls look at it as an opportunity. Let's be smart, Wei Ping; now your feet will be much smaller than we'd dared to hope."

Wei Ping gave no reaction. She seemed not to understand.

But Xing Xing understood perfectly. Stepmother's face appeared transformed into a monster face twisted with this monstrous idea.

Stepmother turned to Xing Xing. "Get me the cleaver."

Wei Ping still gave no reaction.

Xing Xing knew for sure now that Wei Ping didn't understand. If she had understood, she'd have screamed no. Xing Xing didn't move.

"Get it, Lazy One," hissed Stepmother. "It's your fault we had the demon raccoon in the house. And that fish must be a demon too. Get me that cleaver or I'll use it on your face, so everyone will know you invite demons into decent homes."

Xing Xing ran outside. She grabbed the bowl with the beautiful fish that was still waiting at the foot of the jujube tree. She ran with it to the pool, her eyes and nose streaming, and dumped the fish in the water at the very moment she heard Wei Ping's shriek.

9 Xing Xing squatted by the pool, with her right arm tight around her calves and her left hand dangling in the water. Her forehead pressed on her knees. "Mother, Mother, what can I do? Where can I go?"

The beautiful fish sucked at the tip of her thumb.

She turned her head and rested her cheek, instead, on her knees, so that she could look at the fish while she talked to the spirit of her mother. "I didn't mean to bring a demon into the house. I thought I was simply having pity on an unfortunate creature."

The fish now moved to the tip of Xing Xing's index finger.

"But I should have guessed, of course. The wretched spirit of that raccoon was responsible for his misfortune. How could I have trusted him?"

The fish sucked on the tip of Xing Xing's middle finger.

"And I didn't trust him, not really. After all, I

brought the beautiful fish with me out to the jujube trees so he wouldn't eat her."

The fish sucked on the tip of Xing Xing's next finger. Then it moved on to suck at the tip of her pinky. The fish's white scales were without blemish, pure white brightness, like the positive energies of the universe. Father had taught Xing Xing that there were two kinds of energies: the negative *yin* and the positive *yang*. All things needed both: the stillness, darkness, and cold of *yin* as well as the movement, brightness, and heat of *yang*. Without one, the other could not be, for what is brightness without dark? Harmony resulted from a balance of the two.

Xing Xing had always felt more affinity to the *yang* within her than to the *yin,* even though she was a girl, because her own name evoked a sense of brightness. Now she thought about how the animal that most embodied *yin* was the tiger and the animal that most embodied *yang* was the dragon. And this beautiful white fish wanted to become a dragon, so she, too, was more drawn to *yang* than *yin*. Xing Xing and the fish shared a bond.

"I'm glad he didn't eat you," said Xing Xing, moving her face closer to the fish. She sniffled. "But I'm so sad for poor Wei Ping."

A crow cawed, unluckiest of birds. Then another, then the whole flock, out of sight beyond the trees, as though announcing the ill fortune of Xing Xing's family.

Xing Xing looked down at her own naturally small feet. She had always taken pride in them, a pride she kept secret, of course. But now she would have given anything if she could have traded her small strong feet for Wei Ping's big feet before the girl had had them bound. At least with small feet to start with, Wei Ping's ordeal would have been reduced, and maybe her feet wouldn't have given off the stink that drew the demon raccoon to them. Poor, poor Wei Ping.

And, oh, poor, poor Xing Xing, cast out from her family. "Where will I go now? What will I do?" she sobbed.

Xing Xing rested her cheek on her knees again. A girl alone in the world had few choices. Everyone said Xing Xing was pretty. She realized in this moment that she'd secretly harbored the hope that someday Stepmother would decide to find her a husband too. Now that would never happen, and her prettiness could well condemn her to a life without virtue.

She closed her eyes and let the tears slip out

sideways, rolling across the bridge of her nose, across her temple, into her hair. In her sadness she imagined many things. Her head became the carp bowl that sat on the ground beside her feet. She was a frog trapped in the bowl, scrabbling at the slick sides. And now the bowl cracked, and a white wave of water washed her out and away, and it was not the pool she was in, but their great, wide river, which in a flash turned wild and swift and carried her into the upper regions of the Han River, then down down down southward into the giant Yangzi River, with its incessant winds, and out to sea, where no frog could survive. Her skin dried in the salt. Her eyes split. Her fingers curled till they disappeared. She heard screaming.

Xing Xing opened her eyes. Was it her own scream she'd heard?

The afternoon sun was already moving toward evening.

"Get up, Lazy One." Stepmother leaned on a cane. Her cheeks were drawn, but the blood that had covered her face and arms had been washed away and she wore fresh clothing. And, most important of all, there was no knife in her hand, nothing to carry out the threat she'd made in the cave. She didn't even hold a willow switch for beatings.

Xing Xing got to her feet with difficulty. She'd been squatting so long, her legs had cramped into position.

"Go get Master Tang's slave boy. The two of you can carry Wei Ping together. We are going to Master Wu's grave."

Had Stepmother truly forgiven her and accepted her back into the family? And going to Father's grave—that was wonderful. Indeed, nothing could be better at this moment than honoring the spirit of Father. Xing Xing stood stupid, afraid to believe her good fortune.

"Has talking to that evil fish turned you into an idiot?" Stepmother stomped the cane in the dirt. "Hurry, Lazy One."

Xing Xing ran, with spikes shooting up her legs from her still sleeping feet.

"Stop!" shouted Stepmother.

Alas, this fortune had been too good to be true. Xing Xing turned in dismay to Stepmother.

"Come back and take this bowl." She pointed to the carp bowl on the bank of the pool. "Sell it to Master Tang. No, no, sell it to his wife instead. She has a softer heart. She'll lose it in the clutter of her house, and I'll never have to see it again. Get a good price."

The beautiful fish was too large for that bowl now anyway. The fish would be much happier free in the spring-fed pool. Xing Xing came back, bowed once before Stepmother, then picked up the bowl.

"Walk," said Stepmother. "You mustn't break the bowl. But walk as fast as you can. And"—she pointed her cane at Xing Xing—"never say a word to anyone about what happened today. Once Wei Ping is married, we will find a way to explain to her husband. A way that doesn't mention devils."

10 Master Tang's wife, Mei Zi, ran her gnarled finger over the character in the center of the bowl. "Was this your clever idea?"

Xing Xing didn't speak, for to answer would be immodest. Her cheeks went hot. Besides, she didn't want to start a conversation. She had to hurry, for Wei Ping's sake.

"I recognize your calligraphy, of course." Mei Zi looked thoughtfully at the bowl. "It is, indeed, a marvelous bowl." She set it down on the fine bamboo table. "But I have little use for it myself."

Xing Xing pressed her lips together and looked down.

"It would make the perfect gift for my daughter-in-law, however," added Mei Zi after a pause.

Xing Xing looked up with gratitude into the smiling eyes of Mei Zi.

"Let's see how much I can afford for it." Mei Zi

went through an inner door, leaving Xing Xing alone in the central room.

The abundance of superb things—rosewood furniture and elaborately carved jade statuettes and lacquerware in reds and blacks and an engraved walrus tusk—made her stand very straight and tall, her arms pinned to her sides. She knew that breathing alone never broke things, but still, she breathed shallowly. She would move as little as possible, except for her eyes.

In the cave they had good-quality furniture too, though Stepmother had sold anything not absolutely necessary. But even when Father was alive, their belongings had been in nowhere near the abundance found in Master Tang's house. Father liked simplicity—a taste Xing Xing had inherited. And Master Tang was wealthy—something the Wu family was not.

Her eyes moved past the more showy items and slowly took in the line of blue-and-white porcelain bottles on the shelf beyond the table. They were decorated with lines that made pleasing patterns on the rounded sides and at the neck. The fronts were flat, however, and though she couldn't see the backs, she guessed they were as well. On the fronts were ovals with words written from top to bottom. She read, *Asparagus. For the treatment of painful ill-*

nesses in the joints and lower back. The next jar said, *Sesame,* and the next, *Poppies.* Some of the bottles merely said what the cure was, without the ingredient: *Eye remedy; Intestinal calming lotion; Elixir of eight precious ingredients for rescue from danger.* One bottle had no words, but an erotic scene instead, and Xing Xing knew it was one of the aphrodisiacs that she'd overheard women gossip about as they stood in little gaggles around the cart of the occasional visiting doctor. Stepmother never talked about them. But Father had told her that erotic scenes were nothing to be shamed by; rather, they were talismans for good luck, and this was a moment when Xing Xing's family needed all the luck they could get. She stared for several minutes.

On the shelf against the adjoining wall were more bottles, their flat fronts in the shape of octagons, sitting on stands and with little necks that held paper and cork stoppers. These had the *yin-yang* symbol in the center with a series of three lines going out to the sides at intervals, like spokes. There were so many bottles and they were lined up so precisely straight that Xing Xing had that same sensation she felt when looking at the endless horizon of the sea in so many of Master Tang's paintings—that sensation of being as tiny as a dust mote. All the bottles, on both shelves, had a funny little character at the top that Xing Xing had never seen before.

"We bought them when a state pharmacy in the big city closed," said Mei Zi. She had come back without Xing Xing noticing, the girl had been so absorbed in studying the bottles.

"Do you have anything for pain in the feet?" asked Xing Xing.

Mei Zi laughed. "Oh, they're not full. We know nothing about the practice of medicine, dear girl. Master Tang and I enjoy them just as objects of beauty. Here, come take a look at these." She led Xing Xing to a small table in a corner that held a low, wide bowl.

Xing Xing immediately recognized the bowl as one her father had made. In it was a pile of something she was familiar with—pottery shards. Their jagged edges brought back the image of Wei Ping's bone ends. She had to hurry.

Mei Zi held up a shard with a frog pattern on it. "This is old. I don't know how old, but hundreds and hundreds of years. Perhaps even thousands. It was found way down south, in the Dongting Lake area of the Yangzi River. The artistry is crude, but it may have been sacred to the people who used it."

The frog had a round back with two stripes down the center and dots on either side in perfect reflection. Despite the urgency of the moment, Xing Xing couldn't help but feel delight. She imagined the frog hopping at the muddy edge of the river. "It's lovely," she said.

Mei Zi opened her hand. It was full of small coins of cast copper. She looked Xing Xing over, then she reached into the folds of her bodice and took out a cloth purse. "Help me open this, please, for my fingers cannot work the clasp anymore." Xing Xing opened the purse, and Mei Zi poured the coins into it.

Xing Xing was embarrassed that in Stepmother's and her haste, she'd forgotten to bring a purse. "I will return the purse quickly," she said.

"I have others. You can keep it. And you'll need something to fill it after you've given your stepmother this money." Mei Zi's eyes discreetly went toward the bowl of pottery pieces, then back to Xing Xing's face. "Pick the one that pleases you best."

Xing Xing shook her head. "I couldn't. Something so old and fine. Never."

"But that's exactly why you should have one," said Mei Zi, and her face spoke plainly her sincerity.

"Many people consider this junk, but you value it properly. Choose one."

Xing Xing didn't dare put her hand in the bowl; she let her eyes do the searching. And there it was—a small part from the fluted mouth of what had clearly once been a large jar. It must have been a water jar, for this one piece held two animal images: a frog, like the one on the shard Mei Zi had shown her, and a beautiful carp.

11 The three of them gathered before the shrine in the innermost cavern. Stepmother solemnly read off the names of their recent ancestors painted on the wooden tablets. Then she uncovered the bowl of rice that Xing Xing had prepared. Xing Xing straightened in surprise, for Stepmother had added the delicate white flesh of a snake, arranged in a graceful swirl on top of the grains. This was a hearty meal, for sure. The ancestors should feel well cared for.

"Most worthy ancestors," said Stepmother, "may you do the favor of listening to my meager voice. Other beliefs are popular today even here in the north—Buddhism and Daoism. But we are still followers of Kong Fu Zi, and we never forget that. We revere antiquity and the sages. We place family above all."

Wei Ping appeared not to hear anything. It wasn't clear she knew what was going on. She rolled her head from side to side. She clasped her arms across her chest, and her fingers dug into the flesh of her upper arms.

But Xing Xing listened closely. Though she'd heard this invocation many times, the gravity of adult voices when they approached the ancestral shrine always impressed her.

"We seek your assistance," said Stepmother. "We long for your protection. Only with it may we avoid misfortune." She bowed her head. "Bless the children of Master Wu. Though they be girls and essentially worthless, they are the only descendants of this family. You are such generous and wise ancestors that you look after even the most unworthy of us. For this we thank you. Every good thing that happens to us happens because of you."

Stepmother left the room. She came back a few moments later followed by Master Tang's slave boy. She draped one of Wei Ping's arms around the boy's neck and the other around Xing Xing's. Wei Ping still gave no indication of knowing what was going on. But when the boy and Xing Xing each took one of her legs, she let out a hair-raising yowl and her face twisted in such excruciating pain that they almost dropped her.

"We must go as fast as you can manage," said

Stepmother, picking up a sack and hobbling on her heels behind them. "To Master Wu's grave. Hurry."

Father's grave was at the edge of a group of graves, all of the Wu family. Xing Xing and the slave boy set Wei Ping on the ground beside the grave. The girl immediately cried out, "Stop this pain, Father, I beg you. I beg all my ancestors," and she collapsed in sobs.

Stepmother sank to her knees, then sat back with her feet tucked to the side and arranged her sackcloth around her knees demurely. "Forgive the girl for speaking so bluntly. Physical misery makes children forget to show proper respect." She reached into the sack and took out candles. "Help me, Xing Xing," she said.

Being addressed by her right name was a privilege Stepmother afforded Xing Xing only when they performed the rituals of ancestor worship. Xing Xing wondered if perhaps Stepmother believed that if she acted kind at these times, Father's ghost wouldn't know how she treated her stepdaughter at other times. Such a belief would be absurdly naïve—spirits could be anywhere, at any time. You had but to call out to a spirit of a close ancestor and it would come to you if it knew where you were. That's why it was so important to speak to the spirits and let them know when you went anywhere unexpected.

Together Stepmother and Xing Xing stood the candles in the trough of river sand dug at the foot of the grave for just that purpose. Then Stepmother handed Xing Xing sticks of incense. Xing Xing placed these in the stoneware bowl of sand right on the center of the grave.

Stepmother nodded to Master Tang's slave boy. The boy struck the flints and lit a long stick, which he used to light the candles and the incense. The incense smoke rose in spirals, inviting ghosts and spirits.

"When our daughter spoke today of remarriage, she was terribly mistaken," said Stepmother in a wavering voice. "I would commit suicide before I'd enter another man's bed. See how I wear the sackcloth of mourning? See how mine is unhemmed and ugly? I will wear it a full three years, I promise." Then she added more forcefully, "When you died, we did a proper ceremony. We said the right words to help you find your way to your ancestral home. We burned maple and white spruce. We wrapped an ox's horns in bamboo wreaths and sacrificed it. We did everything right, everything." She shook her head. "See? There's no cause for any spirit to hide under our roof and haunt us. All I wanted then, all I want now, is to give you pleasure. I know that not producing a male heir was a terrible blow for you. But if you will help Wei Ping find a husband, I will take her second son and raise him as though he were yours. He will be accepted as a legitimate heir to your household. I will get her husband to agree to this somehow. I promise you, my dearest husband." Her voice was as humble as that of an orphaned child, and Xing Xing felt like crying for her, who had lost her husband, for Wei Ping, who would lose her second son, for all of them. She wiped at her running nose.

Now Stepmother stood. She picked up the sack from the ground and turned it upside down, shaking hard. Paper money fluttered onto the grave.

Xing Xing swallowed her surprise.

But Wei Ping didn't. "Can we afford all that?" Her broken voice trembled in fear.

"Hush," said Stepmother. She took a lit candle and set the paper money on fire.

Xing Xing shielded her eyes from the smoke. It was better that Stepmother burned paper money than left copper coins, she knew, for there were bandits who stooped so low as to rob money left on graves. But while burned money might prove how much Stepmother revered the Wu ancestors, Xing Xing couldn't understand how it would give pleasure to Father's spirit. Xing Xing knew what pleasured Father better than anyone. She'd been thought-less not to bring a flower or a feather or a colored pebble—for Father enjoyed little objects of beauty, the simpler the better. It was still Xing Xing's job to care for Father; Mother had entrusted her with that sacred job. Alas, she had nothing to give him. She was letting him down again, just as she had let him down the day he died. He had fallen into a deep ravine when a boulder gave way under him. He died instantly. Certainly, he had no dying words, so Xing Xing had no chance to listen to them as Mother had asked her. Nevertheless, something inside her had failed, for a person who is about to die gives off an aura that those who love him should be able to sense. Xing Xing had not noticed the aura of death around Father that morning. She had noticed only that the one gray hair she'd spotted on his head before then now had a partner. How sad to let him down again—to have empty hands.

But, oh, she did have something after all. She pulled on the string that went down the inside of the front of her bodice and surreptitiously fished out the purse Mei Zi had given her. She untied it from the string and caressed the pottery shard with the frog and fish through the silk of the purse. Stepmother and Wei Ping were absorbed in their own thoughts and didn't notice her actions. The slave boy kept sneaking looks at her, but he was no threat, she was sure. She buried the purse in the sand trough.

She had owned the lovely shard of pottery for only a matter of hours. But at least she'd always know that Father was enjoying it. Besides, she had the real carp as her friend, and that was better by far than any number of carp images.

Xing Xing warmed at the thought of the fish being her friend. She had never had real friends other than Wei Ping. Girls her age distrusted her because of her education. It seemed they were confused and almost embarrassed by the way her life had taken a turn so different from theirs. She understood, and so she never lingered—hurrying past them as though intent on important errands. She used to think wistfully of them. But now she had the fish.

She bowed one more time. Then, before she left, she tilted her cheek toward Mother's grave, as if to give and receive a tender touch. That's all Mother's grave really needed, for Xing Xing knew that Mother's spirit didn't stay in her grave much. Mother's spirit liked to follow Xing Xing about.

12 Wei Ping sat on the *kang* rocking back and forth in the pain that seemed to keep increasing. She droned a tuneless hum. Xing Xing wanted to hug her but feared hurting her more. So she gave her half sister's hand a light squeeze to say good-bye, and the unnatural heat of Wei Ping's skin scared her. She walked to the small opening in the four bamboo walls that now surrounded the *kang*. That opening led to a little corridor of bamboo on both sides that made a sharp turn before opening into the main cavern room.

Only the day before, under Stepmother's guidance, Master Tang's slave boy and Xing Xing had built the square screen around the *kang* and that little, crooked corridor. Demons cannot turn corners. Any demon who entered the corridor would be stopped short at that sharp turn. Wei Ping was safe so long as she stayed at the *kang*. She had even slept there the night before, and she would sleep there for the foreseeable future.

Her bed was not empty, however. In the center was a plate of fatty pork. Demons were greedy, and once they got busy eating, they'd forget about their original prey. For good measure here and there around the cave Stepmother had placed boxes with crickets and hard-shelled beetles that glowed in the dark, all of which she'd ordered Xing Xing to catch for her. Demons loved to play with such things.

Xing Xing was glad for all of Stepmother's precautions, for she wanted Wei Ping to be safe in her absence. She picked up the sack of green jujube dates. It was heavy, but not so heavy as to slow her down terribly. Stepmother had been careful in that regard.

"The *lang zhong* will leave the neighboring village soon," said Stepmother. "So you must hurry. If he has already gone by the time you get there, follow him to the village beyond."

Xing Xing had never gone beyond the neighboring village. "How will I know the way?"

"Ask, Lazy One," barked Stepmother. Then she seemed to relent a little. Her face softened. "No one will try to stop you when they see that all you have is a sack of unripe dates. And you are of such a small frame that within your loose dress, no one will guess you are anything but a child. You will pass unmolested. Your ancestors will protect you. You understand what you are to do?"

Xing Xing nodded. Stepmother had repeated the instructions too many times. Xing Xing could never forget them.

"You must succeed," said Stepmother. "You must. And in the meantime, I will allow no demons to come near my daughter. I will fight with my very life."

Xing Xing stepped out into the haze that precedes the morning of what will be a hot, hot day. She walked down the hill, feeling Stepmother's eyes on her back. When she was sure she was out of sight, she took off the sack and hid it in some bushes. Then she snuck back to the spring-fed pool.

"Beautiful fish," she called.

The fish came to the surface of the water, as she had done every morning and every evening since Xing Xing had returned her to the pool. Usually, Xing Xing offered the fish a bit of her meal, which she would lovingly save. But now she had nothing. In fact, she didn't even have a piece of fruit for her own future meal. Stepmother had wanted her to go empty-handed, hoping that hunger would spur her to do her errand as quickly as she could.

"I'm going to the neighboring village," said Xing Xing. "I wish I could explain to you, so you wouldn't wonder where I was." The day before when she had visited Father's grave, she'd made the same announcement. That hadn't been so worrisome, though, since Father's spirit understood everything. Her brow furrowed. But then she smiled. "At least you won't be hungry, that's obvious. Look how much larger you've grown already. This pool must be full of good fish food." Indeed, the fish was as long as Xing Xing's arm. "I bet I'll miss you more than you'll miss me. Don't forget me, please. I'll return to you, I promise."

Xing Xing scurried back to the bushes and picked up the sack of dates. "Mother," she sang out, "come with me. Stay with me." She followed the road along the river valley toward the neighboring village.

She passed a furniture maker and his two slave boys tapping a lacquer tree in the predawn light. The furniture maker moved swiftly, applying dozens of layers of lacquer to a wooden screen before the air could harden the sap beyond usefulness. His engraving knife flickered here and there in the first rays of sun. There used to be a lacquer screen like that in the cave. They stood it behind the oven, since lacquer is resistant to cooking steam and heat. Father had said it would outlive them all. Xing Xing didn't know who owned it now.

The early summer sun flooded the land in an instant. Already it baked the back of Xing Xing's shoulders. She thought briefly of the cool of the cave. But she had to hurry to the village—hurry for Wei Ping's sake.

When she was younger, she used to go to this village a couple of times a month with Father. Other girls stayed with their mothers, but Father liked to take Xing Xing and Wei Ping out to see a bit of the world. After he died, there was no one to take her anywhere. These days the only time she even visited their own village was on an errand for Stepmother. So a flush of excitement went up her arms and chest as she finally came to the first store.

Outside some men had set up a low fence of sticks. They surrounded it and shouted at whatever was in the center. Xing Xing wiggled through the crowd and peeked. Two huge cockroaches attacked each other. Near the fence were small cages, some with more roaches, others with crickets and grasshoppers. She understood immediately: These men were betting on the fight. And once they were through with the roaches, they would bet on cricket fights and grasshopper races. Father had bet sometimes too. Xing Xing always hated it when he bet, because if he lost too much money, Stepmother would go into a screaming fit. Any extra money should have gone for Wei Ping's dowry, after all. Xing Xing watched as the smaller roach bit the head off the other. A cry of triumph went up from some of the men.

Xing Xing backed away. She went into the store, where folds of material for making clothing were arranged on tables everywhere. But this store also sold signs with sayings on them to hang in homes or in places of business. She read, *Dragon and phoenix manifest good fortune. Marriage celebrations arrive at the house.* Wouldn't Wei Ping love a sign like that? She read, *Business flourishing as far as the four seas. Riches in abundance reaching the four rivers.* Xing Xing wished she had the money to buy that one and bring it home to read to Stepmother; Stepmother would love it.

She approached the shopkeeper with optimism. To her utter dismay, she learned that the *lang zhong,* true to his name, had already wandered off to a town downriver, a much larger town than this village, to offer his medicinal services. That town was half a day's walk away for a full-grown man. Poor Stepmother would have to fight the demons alone for longer than either she or Xing Xing had anticipated.

13 Without hesitation, Xing Xing started on the road the merchant pointed to. The sun was at its highest point. Sweat soaked through her dress. But she wouldn't give in and rest in the shade of a tree; she had to hurry. A girl couldn't sleep out in the open on her own. Wolves prowled at night. And what if there were tigers in the forest on the other side of the river? Tigers swim. Xing Xing had to reach the *lang zhong* before nightfall.

Boats sailed past on the nearby river, heavy with boxes, some sheltered by woven bamboo canopies and some out in the open. Xing Xing wished she were a bird—maybe a kingfisher or something dramatic like a painted stork. Then she could fly to a boat mast and perch up high, where the air was undoubtedly cooler.

The cicadas kept up a high-pitched scream from the tall trees—the elms and yellow-leaved poplars and hardwood nanmus. White strings of sesame flowers lined the busy road.

After a couple of hours Xing Xing stopped briefly to rub her tired feet. An ox-drawn cart rolled by with a boy running beside it. A rope around the boy's waist tied him to the ox's horns. That's how cruel owners kept their slave boys from running off. The cart slowed to a halt, and the driver waved for her to catch up. "Climb in," said the man, smiling with the few teeth he had left and patting the bench beside him. Despite his mouth, though, he wasn't old enough to be harmless. His bare arms were thick, like Stepmother's. And he looked at her in that way men looked at unmarried women in the village.

"Thank you for your kindness," said Xing Xing. "I'll ride in back."

"With the smelly birds?" said the man in surprise.

"I like them," said Xing Xing, and she threw her sack in among the crates of birds, then had an instant of panic when she realized that if the man wanted, he could take off before she climbed up, and she and her sack would have been parted just like that. She practically threw herself into the cart, knocking askew a stack of crates and making the birds inside squawk furiously, which sent up a din from all the other crates as well.

"What's inside the sack that you value so much?" asked the man.

Xing Xing knew he wouldn't believe her words. So she opened the sack and took out a date.

The corner of the man's mouth twitched upward. "Green dates are of no use to anyone."

"My stepmother likes their bitterness," said Xing Xing. It wasn't a lie, not really. And it offered an irrefutable explanation.

The man shrugged and slapped the back of the ox with his switch. They rolled down the road.

The crates Xing Xing had knocked into held hens, and one held a cock with a crimson comb. But other crates held ducks and geese and swans and quails, the less fortunate headed eventually for people's ovens and the more fortunate for people's private pools, which, like bamboo groves, were abundant the farther south you went. Still others held songbirds, for almost every home Xing Xing had ever visited had a songbird or two in a cage. Her own home had always had songbirds and often mynas. But somehow when the last one died, Stepmother hadn't gotten around to replacing it. Xing Xing had been grateful for that when she'd brought home the blind raccoon kit. How mistaken she'd been. That cage would never house another songbird, for Stepmother had smashed it to pieces and thrown it in the dung heap.

Xing Xing snuggled herself down among the lowest crates. It was stiflingly hot there, nothing like the windblown perch she'd longed for on a riverboat, but at least she was out of the sun.

A hen clucked, and an egg rolled from her onto the bottom of the crate. Xing Xing stared at it. Fresh raw eggs were delicious, and she hadn't eaten since early morning. This bird merchant clearly didn't sell eggs, for there were no boxes of eggs in the cart. And the hen was certainly destined for someone's cooking pot, so she'd never get a chance to raise the chick. That meant no one in the world would miss that egg if she ate it. And Stepmother was wrong—Xing Xing would hurry in her errand no matter what; she didn't need hunger to rush her along. On the other hand, that egg belonged to the man, and surely he would eat it if he knew it was there.

The cart must have hit a gully in the road, for it bumped extra hard. The egg smacked against the side of the crate and cracked. All its goodness slowly oozed out, enjoyed by no one.

After awhile another hen clucked and another egg settled on the bottom of the crate.

Xing Xing worked at the knotted string that held the crate door closed. The bird merchant was smart—he'd wet down the knots. These strings were meant to hold tight until they were cut. But Xing Xing's hands, like her feet, were small, with thin, agile fingers. After a long while she managed to open the crate door. She reached in and grabbed the egg.

A hen pecked her hard and screeched, then the whole crate was screeching.

"What's the problem back there?" called the man.

"No problem," answered Xing Xing, hiding the egg under her cocked knees.

The man stopped the cart. She heard him say, "Get in the back." The next thing Xing Xing knew, the slave boy had climbed in beside her. The rope around his waist was now tied to a side support on the cart.

The boy looked at her. He was as skinny as she was, and his clothes were as tattered. Plus, he was younger. And then there was the matter of that rope. Xing Xing decided it wasn't much of a risk to take. She put the egg in her lap and tapped a hole in one end with her thumbnail. She sucked out half the inside. Then she passed the egg to the slave boy. He finished it and threw the shell out the back of the cart.

That egg was good. And now her stomach woke up and called for more food. She looked around at the other crates. The boy looked too. They shared a duck egg, then another hen egg. Then the boy looked in Xing Xing's sack. He took out a green date and ate it. "Won't you vomit from eating green fruit?" whispered Xing Xing. The boy grinned and ate another. Xing Xing grinned back. After all, she'd seen the size of the medicine jars in Master Tang's house; there were way more than enough dates in her sack to fill as many jars as the wandering doctor might have.

The boy seemed spurred on by Xing Xing's grin. He picked up a hemp stalk that was lying on the floor of the cart. "Want to make a bet? Do you think bad sounds or bad sights frighten chickens the most?"

Xing Xing never made bets, of course. Besides, she knew nothing about chickens. They'd never owned them because Father didn't like their smell. "I have nothing to bet with."

"Come on, you have to have something more than green dates."

"Nothing. I swear."

"All right, then. I'll just put on a show for you." The boy got on all fours with his face very close to a crate. He made a terrible monster face at a hen.

The hen ignored him. He flapped his hands on both sides of his head as he made the face a second time. Still, she ignored him. The boy smiled at Xing Xing. Then he looked back at the hen and chewed noisily on the hemp stalk. *Crack crack crack.* Xing Xing laughed in amazement: It sounded just like a cat eating a chicken, cracking its bones. The chickens in the crate went wild, clucking like crazy things.

"No more of that," shouted the driver.

The slave boy took a small box out of his pocket. He opened it and held it before Xing Xing's face. Translucent rice-colored insects crawled over one another, their short forelegs and long hindlegs intertwining. The boy popped a few in his mouth and raised his brows at Xing Xing. She had never eaten anything live before; she shook her head no. He put the box away, settled back, and closed his eyes, a grin still on his face.

After several hours Xing Xing heard singing. She got to her knees and looked out at a rice paddy, where men worked naked in the waning sun, their backs glistening with sweat. A water buffalo dragged a platform that the men stacked rice stalks on. They were harvesting already. At this rate, maybe they'd even get three plantings in this season.

At the edge of the paddy black-necked cranes walked on stilt legs. They were a common sight at rice paddies; they came to feed on frogs. But Xing Xing spied an uncommon sight too: a cream-colored head, then two neck collars—one green, the other tan, and both with black stripes. It was a golden pheasant. She stood, steadying herself by holding on to a crate. She smiled as she watched the bird poke along, trailing that black tail with gold speckles, until it was out of sight. Then she sat, happy. A pheasant was a good omen for a rice harvest. And maybe that one was a good omen for Xing Xing, too; maybe this journey would end well.

Soon after they passed the paddy, the oxcart turned off the main road onto a country path. What was going on? Xing Xing felt sure that this wasn't the way to the town.

She got to her feet again and unsteadily looked out over an orchard of apple trees as the cart bumped along. "I have to get off," she called to the driver. "I'm going to the town on the main road."

"We're practically there," he called back. "But a man can't sell fowl in the evening. There's a place up here where I like to spend the night, so I can wake early and get into town as the market opens. A girl like you shouldn't be out on your own at this hour, anyway. Your stepmother must not care too much for you." He laughed. "But you're in luck—we'll stop up here a little ways and share a meal. And you can spend the night with me."

"Thank you," said Xing Xing, and she squatted, out of his sight. Her fingers worried the cloth of the date sack. People were basically good, despite the pirates on the seas and the brigands in the mountains. Kong Fu Zi's teachings were clear on that. And what would happen would happen; fate ruled the cosmos. Xing Xing knew all this. But Father had told her that some people were fated to use their heads. And wasn't a fish fated to hide under a lily pad when a shadow crossed her path?

When Xing Xing was sure the driver had turned his attention back to driving, she crawled past the slave boy to the back of the cart. He made no move to stop her. She wished she had something to give him to show her gratitude, but all she had were dates, and he'd already eaten his fill of them. She bowed deep to him. Then she threw her sack over and jumped after it.

She hit the uneven ground hard, bruising both knees and reopening the gash in her arm she'd gotten when she fell from the jujube tree that day the raccoon had attacked Wei Ping. She looked over her shoulder at the cart, expecting that the thud of her fall would have made the driver stop. But the cart kept going. She grabbed the sack and ran back along the path. On both sides now were fields with alternating rows of turnips and cabbages. If she heard the cart slow down, there would be nowhere for her to hide. She ran as fast as she could toward the apple trees, looking back often, as the sound of the wheels grew fainter.

The cart was practically even with another field now, one high with wheat. It was far off, but the path was so straight that if the driver looked back, he'd surely see her.

Xing Xing ran, panting. She came to the apple trees, and at that very moment a cry went up from the slave boy. He pointed out into the wheat field that the cart was now passing by, shouting, "She jumped out and ran that way!"

The man stopped the cart and stood on his seat to get a better look. But he didn't look into the wheat field; he looked back up the path, right at Xing Xing. She ducked into the apple orchard and dashed from tree to tree in the direction of the main road. Branches tore at her skin and clothes.

14 There is an order to guidance. A ruler guides a subject. A father guides a son. A husband guides a wife. An elder guides a younger. A friend guides a friend.

Xing Xing pressed her cheek into the mud of the riverbank, saying these things to herself in a silent litany inside her head. She couldn't actually speak, because her teeth were clamped down hard on the strings of the date sack that was hanging over her shoulder. She was in water from her chest down, but her hands clung to bits of bramble that allowed her to hug the bank. She heard a cart pass on the road. If she lifted herself up, she would be able to see the road easily, because it ran parallel to the riverbank just a little ways uphill from her, and she could check to see if it was the same oxcart she'd just run away from. But she didn't lift herself up. She didn't dare move. She hardly dared breathe. Xing Xing didn't know how to swim. And her grip on the brambles was weakening. At any moment she could get washed away and drown in the Han River. Who knew the river would be so deep even at the edges?

She stared at a bramble leaf just a breath away from her. At this distance she could study every detail of the leaf. A principle of order guided the pattern of veins in that leaf. In every leaf. In everything on earth. And had not Stepmother said her ancestors would protect her? Certainly, it was Xing Xing's job to protect Father, not vice versa. But her other ancestors should be looking after her, guiding her. Somehow they had guided her to this very spot. She must trust in their wisdom.

The mud crumpled from her weight, and the bramble in her right hand came loose. Xing Xing slid downward. But before her face went underwater, there was something cold and smooth under her feet. Had she hit a rock ledge?

She sidled along whatever was underfoot till she came to another, larger bramble, sticking out of the bank. She grabbed it with both hands and pulled herself out, sopping, onto the riverbank. She lay there for several minutes, the date sack at her side now, letting the fact that she had escaped, that she was still alive, become real for her.

There was no one on the road as far as she could see in either direction. She took off her dress—curling to hide her nakedness in case anyone should appear on the road—wrung it out as hard as she could, then put it back on. In this heat it would dry on her back. She walked along the water's edge toward the town.

A plumed egret alighted on a boulder in midstream. Of all the birds, the plumed egret was Xing Xing's favorite. She often mimicked its walk just for fun. It stood tall and white, its black legs straight, its head tilted. The yellow beak moved slowly from one side to the other, but it couldn't be searching for fish, up high on the boulder like that. Egrets are waders. A breeze came up, ruffling the bird's feathers. It turned and faced into the wind. Its feathers lay flat again. Perhaps the bird was a messenger from her ancestors, who she was quite sure now were guiding her. Maybe they were warning her to pay attention to the prevailing winds.

Xing Xing ran to the point on the bank closest to the egret. She was going to call out her thanks when she saw the big fish. Her beautiful fish. It had to be. There were no other fish white as snow, white as pear blossoms. Like in Mei Zi's poem. And in her own poem. She wished she had something to feed it. The fish swam three times around the egret's boulder, each time returning to the bank near Xing Xing. Then she disappeared.

Could she have been a dream? Though the river near Xing Xing's home emptied eventually into the upper regions of the Han River, there was no direct connection between the spring-fed pool and the river. Xing Xing hoped the fish was a dream, for she wasn't sure that a real fish would be able to swim back upstream when Xing Xing returned home. And she was very sure that any fisherman who saw the beautiful fish would go after her with zeal. She loved that fish. She wanted her to live forever.

But these thoughts somehow did not really worry her. Rather, she realized she felt calm again. Things were happening just as they were supposed to happen. She would stay alert and face the wind. "Thank you, Mother," she called. "Thank you, kind ancestors." She walked along the bank, breathing her thanks.

The man in the oxcart had been right; the town was in sight the very next moment. Xing Xing climbed back up to the road and went toward the buildings. It was early evening, but because of the late sun, every-one was still out and about. Children helped women pull laundry down from bamboo poles. The smells of dinner wafted from windows. People rushed around in their last chance to finish chores before evening.

The road transformed quickly into a cobblestone market street. Much of the merchandise resembled common things sold in her own village—vegetables, eggs, meats, fish—as well as newer things she recognized for special health purposes, such as shark fins and bird nests and the claws of nocturnal birds. All were sold by weight—a certain amount of money for each *liang*. But here she also passed tables laden with paws—thick, black pads on the underside and long, curving claws: bear paws. And paws like hands with amazingly long fingers and fur halfway down the back, from orangutans. She saw shining tiger eyes, and antelope and rhinoceros horns. Toads and river salamanders and all kinds of marine creatures were strung on cords like beads.

Outside a door were stacked cages of puppies and cats and so many kinds of monkeys. Two golden monkeys in adjacent cages hugged each other through the bars. The door had long strips of yellow silk attached to the sides, so Xing Xing knew this was a restaurant, though she'd never entered one. Could the monkeys have possibly known? Xing Xing's eyes stung.

She bowed before each merchant and asked the whereabouts of the *lang zhong*. Always the fingers pointed her ahead along the main road. She came to an open square with a temple on one end, its rooftop adorned with statues of turtles and fish and snakes and benevolent dragons. Farmers sold animals in the center of the square. Children climbed on the backs of pigs and fell off, laughing. Xing Xing couldn't help but smile. And the man in the oxcart had lied; many people were still selling fowl in cages at this hour.

A dried spotted serpent coiled like a rope around the neck of one very fat man who was shaking a ring-shaped hollow rattle. Beside him lay a big black dog, asleep on its side in the dust. Behind him was a cart with little bells hanging from the corners, filled with piles of small cloth sacks and rows of porcelain jars like the ones she'd seen in Master Tang's house. His face was wide, with a square chin. This was a lucky face.

Xing Xing bowed low before him. "Honorable Doctor," she said, deeply impressed by how much wisdom must be stored in his huge belly.

The *lang zhong* gave her a quick glance. "You're not sick," he said with a strange accent. "So what's the message, Wet Girl?"

His directness surprised Xing Xing. But then,

an important man like him must know the right way to talk about these things. So she answered in kind: "In my sack are goods that will help you, Most Honorable Doctor. In return, I beg you to come to my home and tend to my sister."

"I take it these 'goods that will help me' do not include coins?" said the man.

Xing Xing shook her head. Stepmother had given her no coins so that she couldn't be robbed. After burning all that paper money, Stepmother needed to be superbly careful.

"Doctors have honorable motives," said the *lang zhong* at last. "We are accountable to a higher power, a supernatural power. Money does not rule us. Nevertheless," he said, "we must eat."

Xing Xing was hungry herself. The eggs had been few and hours before. She licked her bottom lip.

A woman came up and asked the doctor's help for a rash on her arm. He took out a small jade figurine of a feathered creature, mostly bird but part reptilian, and touched it all over. He had the woman touch it too. Then he poured dried leaves from a jar into a square of paper, which he folded securely and handed to her. He told her to burn the leaves and breathe deeply of the smoke. He took her money and sent her on her way.

A man came up next, limping. He described the aches in his bones. The doctor inserted acupuncture needles at strategic points, talking the whole while. The man had brought his own empty jar; clearly, he was used to going to doctors. He got a refill of the elixir he sought and limped off.

And now, as the sun grew weak and the square emptied, it seemed everyone remembered their ailments. A small crowd formed around the doctor. He took the pulse of a woman who complained of depression, and her pulse seemed to give a clear diagnosis. He sold her an amulet with a picture of a man in fighting gear holding a thick club. The words beside the picture said, *If you want a beating, just come.* He told her to wear it around her neck to ward off the sadness demons. Several men, some with mud caked on their calves from working in the rice paddies, lamented flagging sexual desire. The doctor sent them away with various powders to dissolve in rice wine in a small tortoiseshell and drink an hour before making love. A man wanted the ends of his arms to be longer, a woman the ends of her legs to be shorter. The doctor said spells over them and prescribed physical exercises and gave them small white pills. For some patients he read cards as part of the diagnosis; for others he played a fish-shaped drum as part of the cure. He dispensed elixirs, pills, powders, ointments.

Xing Xing squatted on the ground beside the black dog, who had woken and was now sitting patiently, as though studying the sick people. After awhile Xing Xing dared to touch his floppy ear. He licked her hand. So she petted him constantly while she waited for the last sick person to receive his medicine and leave.

At last she stood. "Honorable Doctor," she said, "could—?"

"Call me Yao Wang," he interrupted.

The word meant "medicine king." It seemed an immodest name, even for the very wisest doctor. Xing Xing looked down at her feet in embarrassment for this *lang zhong*'s self-importance.

"Have you heard of Sun Si Miao?" he asked.

Xing Xing shook her head.

"He lived seven hundred years ago and was the best doctor of all time. The people called him 'Yao Wang.' I use his name to honor him, in the hopes that he will guide my hands at work." Yao Wang held both hands out. "Sun Si Miao is responsible for whatever skills these hands have. He traveled with a black dog and"—he leaned down toward Xing Xing—"and with a tiger and a dragon."

Xing Xing jumped backward.

Yao Wang laughed. "I have no tiger or dragon. Only Sheng."

The dog looked at his master when he heard his name. His tail thumped happily on the ground.

"Sheng was the last of a litter when I entered the restaurant. Instead of eating him, I took him home."

Xing Xing smiled. The name Sheng meant "leftover." "Lucky dog," she said quietly.

"Lucky me," said Yao Wang, "for Sheng has many talents."

Xing Xing squatted and wrote the character for the dog's name in the dirt, making it as beautiful as she could.

Yao Wang leaned so far forward, he had to put his hands on his knees to steady himself. He studied the character, then he straightened up. "You're very skilled."

Xing Xing looked down in shame, for she knew she had drawn in the dirt to show off that she, like the dog, had skills.

"Sheng's hungry," said Yao Wang. "It's time to eat."

15 Yao Wang and Xing Xing lay stretched out on the ground behind a house at the very edge of town. The dry rice stalks that Yao Wang had bought from a farmer cushioned their bones. Yao Wang snored in his sleep. Two ropes went around the cart that held his medicines. The end of one was tied around Yao Wang's wrist. The end of the other was tied around Sheng's neck. If anyone should try to disturb the cart in the night, Yao Wang and Sheng would jump up and defend it. That's why the man slept with his worn hemp shoes on.

It was midmonth, and the bright moon lit up everything. The house was surrounded by cassia trees, the shadows of which spread in a fine pattern. Cassia trees can have golden red blooms or moonlight white blooms—Xing Xing knew this. But in the almost cool of night light, these blooms appeared the gray-pink of wet tongues. A wind rose and the shadows stirred.

Xing Xing reached out and rubbed Sheng's side. The dog, too, was still awake, his eyes glistening in the night. He gave a contented grunt in acknowledgement of her hand.

Yao Wang normally stayed at inns or patients' homes. But no patient today had offered lodging in return for services. And when the innkeeper had requested extra money for Xing Xing, the girl had told the doctor that she didn't want him to pay for her and that she'd gladly sleep outdoors, especially if she could take Sheng with her. After all, being beholden to a man in an inn room was a situation any girl should avoid, no matter how honorable the man might appear.

Yao Wang had responded that sleeping outdoors would be a refreshing change, and Sheng needed that now and then. So they wound up here.

Xing Xing's stomach was fuller than it had been since the funeral feast after Father's death. The three of them—man, girl, and dog—had shared a whole roast duck, feet and head included, and finished it all off with steaming, glutinous rice cakes. Every time she went to open her sack to show Yao Wang the green dates and to explain Wei Ping's problem, the doctor had hushed her. He said that a good meal, a good night's sleep, and time would lead her to tell him the whole truth. He didn't want to waste his time listening to partial truths that would result in nonsense. Though Xing Xing felt the pressure of time passing, she had no choice but to practice patience. So she had lain down in silence, listening to the drums of evening that came from the town and then the croaks of the frogs in the rice paddies.

She watched the cassia patterns for hours. Every joint, every muscle of her body was tired. Even her skin was exhausted. She had traveled a long way, but she'd found the *lang zhong*. This much of her journey had been successful. She closed her eyes and yielded to sleep.

In early morning the bells from town woke them. The air was clear. Down in this river valley, summer morning didn't come in the guise of fog. Xing Xing looked around and felt the lack of dragon spruce and azaleas and of cuckoos overhead. The difference in altitude made it feel like she was in a very different world, much farther from home than she knew she really was.

Yao Wang told Xing Xing to guard his cart while he washed himself in the river. He didn't just splash his arms and legs from the bank. He stripped off his clothes right in front of her and jumped in. He swam and went under the water and floated on his back, his great belly shining in the dawn sun. Sheng paddled around him, joyously.

People passed on the street, singing folk songs. They laughed with wonder at the sight in the water, for neither dog nor man had any fear, even when a boat came, bearing boxes for the market. Xing Xing marveled that one who weighed so much as Yao Wang could be lifted so easily by the water, when a small child could disappear below and never be seen again. She walked up and down the bank looking into the water, hoping to see the beautiful fish while she waited for her companions.

When Yao Wang was ready, they wandered over to a side street, where people sold food they cooked outside—boiled or steamed or fried—in wide curved pans that people in Xing Xing's village used only for drying grains. They stood up eating bowls of rice floating in bean curd whey—white rice of the quality Xing Xing had only on holidays. They ate fried dumplings filled with pork liver. They ate fried bread with sugar sprinkled on top. Sheng ate everything Yao Wang ate, just as though the dog were a person.

Then they walked to the square where Xing Xing had found Yao Wang the day before. Patients came quickly, spluttering loudly about their health problems. While Yao Wang tended to them, Xing Xing took a jar from his cart and looked it over. Unlike the jars in Master Tang's house, the name of the medicine was not fired under the glaze of the vessel. Instead, it was written on top in ink. The writing on this jar was unpleasing; in fact, even ugly. The writing on the other jars was just as bad. At the end of every label was the character for *tiger,* which was supposed to ward off misfortune. But the character was so awkward, Xing Xing was sure it had no power at all.

She searched around in the cart for paintbrush and ink. She found a crude brush, a jar of ink powder, and a bowl meant for mixing up the ink. She didn't want to leave Yao Wang for the time it would take to go down to the river for water. So she spit in the bowl and mixed in some powder to make a small amount of ink. She painstakingly scratched away every bit of the lettering on the jar in her hand. She wrote the name of the contents again in her most beautiful calligraphy. She did the same to a second jar, and a third, all the while keeping her activity a secret from Yao Wang. She couldn't wait to see his reaction when he came upon them later.

The rest of the day passed in this way, as did the following three days. While Yao Wang cured patients,

Xing Xing lettered the medicine jars and combed Sheng's long hair with her fingers. They slept on rice stalks each night, and every time Xing Xing tried to talk, Yao Wang hushed her.

On the morning of their fifth day together, Yao Wang said, "Talk today. But only when I can listen." So whenever Yao Wang had a lull in business, Xing Xing talked. She explained that the spirit of Stepmother's mother had told Stepmother that the green dates made good medicine, though Xing Xing confessed that the spirit hadn't told her for which ailments. She revealed that Stepmother wanted Yao Wang to tell everyone that it was Wei Ping who had recognized the medicinal value of the dates, so that she could find a husband. And despite Stepmother's order never to tell anyone, she told him about Wei Ping's feet and about the demon raccoon that she had so grievously erred in bringing home and about the cleaver in Stepmother's hands.

In her whole life Xing Xing had never said so many words to anyone. Yao Wang had been right about the effects of food and sleep and time: Xing Xing told the whole truth. And she loved telling it. The telling made her feel energized and strong, ready for anything.

Yao Wang made no comment as Xing Xing talked. When it came time for the midday meal, Yao Wang bought them fried fish and seaweed. Then they sat in the shade of a jujube tree and munched on the first apples of the season. Yao Wang turned his face to the sky and spit the apple pips in a high arc, like a small child.

"I am a fat man," he said.

There was nothing to say in response to that.

"I wander from village to town to village, as a *lang zhong* must. But I cannot walk on my own, like a skinny man. Instead, I take whatever rides offer themselves. It is not a simple thing with a dog and a medicine cart." Yao Wang finished his apple and wiped his mouth with the back of his wrist. "People need my services. A girl your age understands that surely."

Xing Xing was not sure where this line of thought was leading, but it made her stomach tumble in worry. "My sister needs your services."

"I use alchemy for longevity. I call on male and female spirits to protect inner organs of humans. I exorcise demons by saying spells in two different Indian languages. I draw on astrological calculations so that I can use acupuncture to its greatest efficacy.

My patients need me, pretty Xing Xing. I am cheap, effective, and convenient. What would they do without me?"

"Maybe exorcism would help Wei Ping," said Xing Xing.

"You will make someone a persistent wife." Yao Wang gave a close-lipped smile as he shook his head. "There are always more patients in the next village. I've already passed your way. I cannot return so soon. It would be too hard for me to get there and back here again. The most I can do is give you a balm and teach you how to apply it."

"I'd be afraid of doing it wrong," said Xing Xing.

"That's exactly how I feel each time I meet a new illness," said Yao Wang. "But I will ask the spirit of Sun Si Miao to guide your hand, as he does mine."

Xing Xing worked to keep the disappointment from her face and voice. "May the dates be beneficial for something," she said, tucking the sack into Yao Wang's cart.

"Thank you. I will experiment with them," he said. "If they turn out to be useful as drugs, I will tell everyone that they came to me from a woman and two girls who live in a cave home outside your village. That's the best I can do." He handed Xing Xing a small cloth sack from his cart. "Take the entire bag. Mix a little with soy oil. Rub it all over both of Wei Ping's feet. Then put a dab right on the open wounds. Do this every other day until scar tissue has formed over the missing toes. And hide this sack well—to keep it safe from pickpockets."

Xing Xing kept her head down so that Yao Wang wouldn't notice her dripping nose. She took the sack of powder, bowed, and left.

16 The smell of incense was making Xing Xing woozy. She had entered the temple to pray because she was too miserable to think straight on her own. There were several altars: to heaven, to the mountains, to the rivers, to the moon, to the earth, to the sun, to the soil, and to Kong Fu Zi. She'd gone from one to another, praying. Stepmother would be furious that she'd come home without Yao Wang after taking all this time. The willow switch would get a good workout. And, worst of all, if Xing Xing applied the balm to Wei Ping too thickly or too thinly or without the right amount of oil mixed with the powder, something awful could happen to her half sister. She had been praying for guidance for a long time now. But maybe the dense fog of incense from the large pewter burners was confusing her too much, because she still had no answers.

She couldn't afford to stay here any longer. It was

already afternoon. If she started out right now and kept up a good pace and nothing bad happened, it would take the rest of the day and part of the next to get home. Maybe longer, actually, since she would duck down to the riverbank whenever she heard the clatter of wheels on the road. She would take no more chances with passing oxcarts, no matter how many hours they might shorten her journey.

She went to the doorway of the temple and shielded her eyes from the bright sunlight. An old man sat on the steps eating a bowl of ox intestines. She recognized him by the ringworm on his head—he was one of Yao Wang's patients. When he saw her, he lifted a string of Buddha beads tucked in his waist sash, shook them at her, and pointed into the square. He was pointing at a crowd pressed around Yao Wang and his cart. But, oh, this was not the usual type of crowd. There were two men in uniform, and people were talking angrily. Sheng showed his teeth and growled at a man who held him at bay with a bamboo stick.

Xing Xing ran to Sheng and threw her arms around the dog's neck. She looked back defiantly at the man with the stick.

The man withdrew his stick. "He's not a real doctor—a real *zhong yi*," he said loudly. "If he were a real *zhong yi*, he would send his patients to a state run pharmacy for their medicine. He's nothing but a *lang zhong*. He costs little," said the man, looking around with a challenge in his eyes, "because he's a quack. A wandering quack. A real doctor is thin because he works hard. This man is a load of blubber who hasn't done an honest day's work in his life. Look!" He picked up one of Yao Wang's medicine jars and held it under the nose of one of the officials. "See? There's no national stamp on this jar. No trademark. These are unregulated drugs—phony drugs. How is an honorable man like me supposed to run a decent pharmacy if charlatans are allowed to sell their junk on the streets? I've already lost a week's worth of business because of him."

The crowd of onlookers didn't say anything. Xing Xing recognized several of them as having been patients of Yao Wang that very day.

The official took the jar from the pharmacist's hand and examined it. He rubbed his cheek as he turned the jar this way and that.

The second official leaned over Yao Wang's cart and touched jar after jar. "Some of these jars have different labeling from others," he said. He picked up one of the jars that Xing Xing had written on and tapped on the character Xing Xing had added to each jar in place of the awkward tiger character that had been there before. It was the character that Xing Xing had seen on all the jars in Master Tang's house. "And here's the national trademark."

The pharmacist shut his lips tight, and his cheeks puffed out so big, he looked like he would pop. "He put that trademark on himself! It's not under the glaze; it's on top. You can tell! He did it himself! This is even worse than being a charlatan. This is a crime. According to the Code, he should be beaten with bamboo. Many blows. At least sixty. No, seventy! I'll bare his buttocks myself and hold him down for you."

Men could die from infections in bloodied bottoms, everyone knew that.

"It's my fault, not Yao Wang's." The words burst from Xing Xing in a high squeak.

Everyone looked at her. They whispered to one another. Some of them giggled.

Xing Xing felt the blood drain from her face. She thought she might faint. She leaned on Sheng for support.

"Yao Wang?" said the second official, raising an eyebrow. "That's your name?"

"'Yao Wang' is her pet name for me," said Yao

Wang with a sheepish look. "You know how foolish things can start with a child."

"Well," said the first official, rubbing hard at his cheek, "speak up, girl."

"I scraped off the words and wrote them again. I was trying to make them pretty. I didn't know about the trademark."

"Are you claiming a pitiful little girl like you knows calligraphy?" asked the second official.

Yao Wang's eyes instantly brightened. "She's been learning—but slowly. Compare the lettering." He held out two jars, one with the ugly lettering and one with Xing Xing's writing. "Which is that of a state representative and which is that of a mere girl?"

The second official, the one who had tapped his finger on the trademark, nodded vigorously. "This is a girl's work." He pointed at the jar with the ugly lettering. "When she copied, she failed to copy the trademark. Just as you would expect from a girl."

"We must not be too harsh on her," said Yao Wang. He shot Xing Xing a hard look that made her feel like she'd been slapped. Then he looked at the officials and smiled sweetly. "Kong Fu Zi is the master teacher of us all," he said humbly. "And Kong Fu Zi says that lack of talent in a woman is a virtue."

The words bit like ants in Xing Xing's ears.

"That's right," said the first official, still rubbing his cheek. "Common sense should guide us in this, as in all social matters—common sense and the teachings of Kong Fu Zi. Mistakes by females shouldn't come under the Code. This is a matter properly between a father and his errant daughter. Not a matter for us."

"Even if the daughter wrote the ugly letters," said the pharmacist quickly, "the jars with the other letters and the stamp are counterfeit. They're not under the glaze. The father is culpable."

"I admit my guilt," said Yao Wang.

Everyone looked at him now. And again the crowd whispered.

"When a jar is empty," said Yao Wang in a voice so soft that everyone had to strain to hear, "a poor man reuses it for whatever suits his needs. A label on top of the glaze can be changed to match the new contents, one under the glaze cannot." He bowed deeply. "Poverty. This is the crime I am guilty of."

"Poverty has never been a crime in China," said the second official, "and our new emperor would be aghast at the idea. He was a peasant himself as a boy. And a beggar, at that. Everything's different now. Government officials are chosen by merit these days, not birth or wealth. I took a civil service examination to get this post." He puffed out his chest.

"But listen to this *lang zhong*'s accent," said the pharmacist. "He isn't from around here. He's probably not even from this province. He's a wanderer, for sure."

The first official put the jar he was still holding back into the cart. He rubbed his cheek. "This is a new dynasty. The reign of Hung Wu values national unity over all else. There's no place for pride in one's native locality over pride in the empire. Besides, the man has clearly lived here a long time—his daughter talks just like you or me."

Yao Wang took a small metal tube out of the cart. "Would you like me to help with that toothache?" he asked the first official.

The man stopped rubbing his cheek and smiled. "A good diagnostician," he said. "But this is a large town; we have three *zhong yi*s, in fact. My whole family goes to Master Si Ma whenever we have problems."

"No charge," said Yao Wang.

"Well, in that case . . ."

"Wait," said the pharmacist. "He's nothing but a *lang zhong*. He doesn't know anything. He should at least have to pay in copper coins to get out of his punishment."

"Being a wandering doctor is no crime," said the second official, "so long as he sells state-regulated drugs, which this doctor does. Punishing a man for what he has not been prohibited from doing is inhumane. The matter is settled." Then he turned to Yao Wang. "It seems some people don't want you in town. My advice to you is to leave, the sooner the better. Small villages will be more welcoming."

Yao Wang bowed. "Wise counsel," he said.

The crowd watched as Yao Wang set in place the acupuncture needles that would control the pain and then neatly extracted the first official's rotten tooth. Only the pharmacist didn't stay for the show.

17 "Where do you think you're going?" whispered Yao Wang out of the side of his mouth. He caught Xing Xing by the elbow.

"Home, of course," said Xing Xing.

"Your home is my home," said Yao Wang. "Have you forgotten that you're my daughter? So long as anyone in this town is watching, we must stay together."

"Then you have to come back to my cave," said Xing Xing, "because that's where I'm going. Wei Ping has been waiting long enough." She pulled herself free and took a few steps in the direction of the road out of town.

Yao Wang muttered angry words Xing Xing was forbidden to say. Then he called out, "Okay, but not that way. To the docks." He took the long handles of the cart in each hand and pulled it behind him; it jingled as it bumped over stones. Sheng walked at his left side. Xing Xing fell into step on the other side.

Yao Wang stopped at the first boat they came to. "Are you heading upriver or down?" he called to the captain.

"Up."

"Then this girl's coming with you."

"No," said Xing Xing in Yao Wang's ear. "I've never been on a boat. I can't even swim."

"Quiet," Yao Wang whispered back. "You'll take this boat upriver, I'll take another downriver. It's the best way to travel."

Before Xing Xing could protest more, the captain spoke, "Not so fast," he said. "We don't generally carry passengers. How much have you got to pay?"

"Think how striking your sails would be with some fine words beautifully painted on them. This girl is a scribe. She won't disappoint you."

"Is that so?" The captain tilted his head at Xing Xing. "How did you come to learn such a thing?"

"My father taught me," said Xing Xing.

"Well, I see you're taking my advice," came a voice from behind them. The second official stood on the dock.

"Wise counsel should never be ignored," said Yao Wang to the official.

"Take good care of them," said the official to the captain.

The captain looked confused. "Them?"

"Captain," said Yao Wang quickly, "tell your men to be specially careful as they load my cart onto the boat, so nothing spills."

"You're coming too?" said the captain. "What about your fare?"

"I can cure skin blemishes." Yao Wang pointed to a boat worker with open sores on his arms. "And clouding of the eye." He pointed to another worker who looked back blankly from two whitened eyes. "And I can expel worms." He pointed at all the men and laughed. "None of these problems are grave yet. But if you let them continue, it will be far harder to cure them."

"Is the dog friendly?" asked the captain.

"Except to those who mean harm to me or the girl," said Yao Wang.

"I mean to cats," said the captain. "We have our share of ratters on board."

"He's a well-mannered dog," said Yao Wang. "When do we set sail?"

So Xing Xing found herself going on her first boat ride, not on a *sampan* for passengers, but on the deck of a cargo boat, beside an ill-tempered Yao Wang. While

Yao Wang treated his patients, who did, indeed, turn out to be all the men on the boat, Xing Xing breathed deep of the river air, invoking its wetness to guide her hand, then painted her calligraphy on an extra sail.

But it wasn't merchant words, announcing what the boat carried. Not at all. It was a poem. The captain turned out to be a man of letters. When Yao Wang showed his surprise at that, the captain looked offended. "The Mongols have been driven out of China, don't you know that?" he said. "Hung Wu's huge military keeps them outside our borders, so men like you and me can turn our attentions to the finer matters of life."

He recited to Xing Xing several poems that he had composed. Together they chose the one that she painted onto the sail.

> *Wood slipping through waters*
> *Wind in passion with sails*
> *Many-layered mountains hold red trees*
> *Some are gone*
> *Some have returned*
> *I grow used to the search for madness*

Though it had no rhyme, Xing Xing liked this poem because it started with such familiar thoughts and ended in such a surprising way. She spent much of the voyage watching for signs of madness in the captain.

At one point the captain smiled down at her work. He squatted beside her and said, "If you fall into water, you may still be saved. But if you fall down in literary matters, there is no life left for you." She thought this might be a sign of madness, but maybe Mei Zi would be sympathetic to such a thought— poetry was so dear to her. It was possible, at least.

At another point the captain actually sat on the deck beside her. He held a small bundle wrapped in lotus leaves. She breathed in the clean smell as he peeled away the leaves and offered her some of the salted meat inside. Then he showed her a mirror that he kept in a wooden box. Its frame was carved with all kinds of sea creatures. He made faces at himself in the mirror. Xing Xing laughed. But the captain wasn't satisfied. He wanted Xing Xing to make faces in the mirror too. She showed her teeth. The captain wasn't satisfied. She showed her teeth and pushed her nose to one side with her finger. He still wasn't satisfied. She showed her teeth and pushed her nose to one side and wrinkled her brow and stuck out her tongue. The captain slapped her on the back in congratulations and left her alone to continue with her work. Perhaps that episode was a sign of madness. But then Xing Xing remembered the slave boy in the oxcart making faces at the hen. Who knew what true madness really was?

The boat tacked back and forth across the river. Whenever there was too long a lull in the breeze, the men took to the oars. And whenever the breeze was steady, the men drank rice ale till they stumbled. When Xing Xing watched them in alarm, Yao Wang told her they were right to drink so much; alcohol kept down gum disease and other illnesses.

Xing Xing worked hour after hour to make her calligraphy as fine as a poem deserved. It was hard, because she'd never had to make such large lettering before. As she worked she refused to think about the pharmacist's words—the way he had accused Yao Wang of being a charlatan. The balm Yao Wang had given her had to work. There was no other possibility she could bear considering. And she avoided looking at the water, for the fear of drowning clutched her throat. But every now and then she had to peek. A few times she was sure she saw a shadow of translucent silvery white just below the surface.

Xing Xing ran up the hill toward her cave. She was alone again. The boat had docked at night, and when the crew punted the boat away from the embankment in the morning, Yao Wang, Sheng, and the medicine cart were long gone. Xing Xing had had to spend the entire day following the captain around, because the looks the crew gave her once she was all alone frightened her more than whatever form of madness the captain was seeking. The noisy surging of the river, which had seemed exciting the day before, now seemed almost brutal, the sloughing of the wind almost ominous.

It was now early evening. Travel by boat against the current was easier than walking, but unfortunately just as slow. She'd been gone so long. The closer Xing Xing got to the cave, the faster she ran.

She opened the squeaking door. Though the summer light still shone outside, the cave was dark inside. The air was stale.

"Go away, demon!" screeched Stepmother from

behind the bamboo screen around the *kang*.

"It's me—Xing Xing," said the girl. She left the door open, and in the dim light it afforded, she made her way through the bamboo corridor and turned into the small area surrounding the *kang*. A thick stench stopped her as firmly as though she'd met a stone wall. Her eyes slowly adjusted to the darkness.

Stepmother sat with her arms wrapped protectively around Wei Ping on the *kang*. Their hair hung down stringy. Their eyes burned at her out of haggard faces.

"Is that truly you?" asked Stepmother in a thin voice.

"Yes. Truly."

Stepmother got unsteadily to her feet. "Where's the *lang zhong*?"

"He wouldn't come," said Xing Xing. "He said that he'd already been this way and that people in other villages need him now."

"And the dates?" Stepmother hobbled around Xing Xing, touching her here and there. Her breath reeked so badly that Xing Xing had to fight to keep her nose from wrinkling. "You gave him the dates anyway?" the woman shrieked.

Wasn't that what she was supposed to do? Xing Xing looked down at her feet in confusion.

"Lazy girl!" Stepmother smacked Xing Xing on the top of her head. It was not a hard blow, but Xing Xing hadn't braced herself against it, so it knocked her to the floor. "You took all these days for nothing!"

Xing Xing pulled the small sack of powder Yao Wang had given her from inside the bodice of her dress. "Medicine," she said, holding it up.

Stepmother narrowed her eyes and put her face close to the sack. Then she snatched it. She sat on the *kang,* and her trembling hands fumbled with the knot.

"Hurry," said Wei Ping. She leaned sideways, putting her weight on one hand; with the other, she clutched Stepmother's arm. "Hurry."

Stepmother picked at the knot ineffectually. Sweat beads formed at her hairline, catching what little light there was. They dripped into her eyes. A brittle note of frustration whistled from between her teeth. Wei Ping poked her finger into Stepmother's arm as the woman worked. Poke poke poke poke— never taking her eyes from the little sack. The two of them seemed demented.

From her position on the floor, Xing Xing looked around. The chamber pot in the corner of the screened area had overflowed. Pits and cleanly gnawed bones had been shoved into a small pile. The water bucket was empty. The stove fire had gone out.

She got to her feet and took the sack of powder from Stepmother, who looked at her passive and dumb now, as though the woman were somewhere else, beyond the present, beyond reaction. Wei Ping was still poking her mother, but aimlessly, without a goal. She didn't even glance at her half sister.

Xing Xing walked outside. She climbed the little steps carved into the side of the cave and rolled the rock from the window, letting the mix of weak sun and moon cascade inside. She went back into the enclosure around the *kang* and took the bucket and went down to the pool and brought back fresh water. She undressed her half sister and her stepmother, discreetly averting her eyes, grateful to find them both cool to the touch, though noticeably thinner. She washed them thoroughly, but she didn't yet touch Wei Ping's bandages. She dressed them in clean clothes. She scoured their teeth with river sand. She scrubbed the *kang*. She swept the floor and emptied the chamber pot and washed every surface with rice vinegar. She gathered wood and fanned a fire with the big bamboo fan and got the stove going and made a gruel from rice powder, which she ladled into bowls, then fed them, spoonful by spoonful. She washed their filthy clothes and strung them just outside the door to dry. She went down the hill in what was now the deep of night and picked early wild chrysanthemums and brought them back and boiled them in water. Then she handed Stepmother and Wei Ping bowls full of the yellow chrysanthemum broth and told them to drink.

Through all this, Stepmother and Wei Ping obeyed Xing Xing as though they were small children. They now rested docilely on the *kang*, stretched out side by side, propped on pillows that Xing Xing had taken from Stepmother's bed. Moonlight made them appear ghostly.

Xing Xing lit enough candles so that she could see well. She poured soy oil into a small bowl and mixed in some of the powder from the sack Yao Wang had given her. She lay clean cloth on the *kang*, at the ready. And, finally, she sat at Wei Ping's feet and unwrapped the bandages from one, bracing herself against what she might find.

The white, distorted foot dripped no blood. The bone ends were as exposed as when the raccoon had first bitten the toes off, but they were no longer ragged. They'd been cut straight with the cleaver. Xing Xing washed the foot and rubbed off the fine slough of dead skin. She gently smeared a thin coat of the balm over the entire foot. Then she put a dollop on the spots where the toes were missing. She worked quickly, remembering what Stepmother had said about blood returning to the foot if the bandages were off too long. She folded the foot under, as she'd watched Stepmother do so many times, and bound it tightly in a clean cloth. Then she tended the other foot the same way. Again the two biggest toes were missing, cut cleanly off.

Wei Ping made no noise as Xing Xing tended her feet. Not even a whimper.

Xing Xing took the half-empty bowls of chrysanthemum broth from the hands of Stepmother and Wei Ping and told them to sleep now.

They shut their eyes.

Xing Xing stood watching them breathe. Until this point she had worked automatically with an unflagging energy. Now it left her. She blew out all the candles but one, which she used to light her way down the hill to the pool. She got on her knees, weary and drained, and leaned forward. She dipped her whole face into the cool water.

Mother's lips brushed her forehead.

Xing Xing lifted her head out of the water and opened her eyes. The white fish glowed soothing moonlight. So the beautiful fish hadn't come down the river after all. She had been safe here in the pool all along. Xing Xing let her clothes drop to the ground. She slipped into the pool and held tight to the side. The fish swam under her, smooth and cold, cold and smooth, like what she'd felt under her feet in the river when she escaped from the man in the oxcart. She knew the fish would never let her drown. She let go of the side and went under, then came up and found that if she moved her arms and legs slowly, she could go wherever she wanted—she could swim—and what a wonderful, effortless joy swimming was.

The two of them circled around each other like white ribbons, making the water swirl behind them. They slid past each other, touching wholly, like mother and child. And at last Xing Xing understood. Oh, she should have known all along: The beautiful fish was the reincarnation of Mother. They were together again, at last.

They swam till Xing Xing found she was almost falling asleep in the water. Still, she didn't want to leave her fish mother. She never wanted to leave her fish mother. She never wanted this joy to end. She climbed out and slept on the bank. Night air patted her dry. The fingers of one hand dangled in the water, twitching now and then as the fish glided by.

19 Yao Wang was no charlatan and the spirit of Sun Si Miao must have guided Xing Xing's hand in mixing the medicine, for by the end of a month, scar tissue had formed on both of Wei Ping's feet and she no longer moaned in pain. The girl hobbled like her mother now, going around and around the cave. She had the bamboo screen put outside, she was so sure there were no demons plaguing her anymore. She woke early and she stayed up late, and her energy increased by the day.

Stepmother, likewise, grew optimistic. She looked with satisfaction at the shrinking size of Wei Ping's feet, and she pulled out the dress she had started making for her months before and worked at finishing it up. She took to going into the village again, to chat with friends and hope for news of a suitable son-in-law.

One morning when the girls woke, Stepmother was standing in the center of the main room rubbing her elbows in excitement. "I'm going to the furniture maker at the edge of the village," she announced.

"What for?" said Wei Ping. "I like it better this way. The cave is spacious." She moved her hands around, indicating the spots that used to have furniture. Stepmother had sold anything extra. "Clutter only provides things for me to stumble over."

"This won't be clutter. We need it."

"If we truly need it, don't go to that furniture maker. He's a poor craftsman. Go to the better one in the center of the village."

"The one I'm going to is cheaper, and what we need made can be crude, so long as it's functional."

"What do we need made?" asked Wei Ping.

"You'll see," said Stepmother with a sly smile. "The annual cave festival is coming up soon. We have to be ready."

Xing Xing had practically forgotten about the cave festival. It was a wonderful event. The whole village celebrated it together, not just the people who lived in the cave homes. It took place in Xing Xing's favorite park.

They ate a breakfast of rice toasted to a crunchy golden brown. Then Stepmother left in a hurry.

When Xing Xing picked up the water bucket and prepared to go to the pool, Wei Ping called out, "Take me with you."

Though Wei Ping was thin, she was much larger than Xing Xing and therefore weighed more. This reality, however, was not something to point out. "I could never manage you and the water bucket at the same time. I'd spill every drop," said Xing Xing diplomatically.

"I'll walk, of course," said Wei Ping. "We just have to go slowly."

"The hill is steep," said Xing Xing.

"Take me with you," pleaded Wei Ping. "I have to practice walking so that I can have fun at the cave festival too. Please take me with you, Sister."

Xing Xing knew Wei Ping was manipulating her by calling her "Sister." But she couldn't help her reaction. She smiled, and the girls slowly made their way together down to the pool.

As Xing Xing approached the water, her beautiful fish mother surfaced and rested her head on the bank. Xing Xing knelt and fed the fish leftovers from breakfast, as she did every morning.

"What a remarkable fish," said Wei Ping, coming up behind her.

The fish quickly dove and disappeared.

"Didn't you recognize her?"

Wei Ping looked at Xing Xing, then her eyes

widened. "But you can't mean that's the same fish that used to swim in the bowl on the *kang* beside me."

"The very same," said Xing Xing.

"But that's delightful," said Wei Ping. "Our fish! And she's grown miraculously. She's longer than an adult man."

The girl was right. Xing Xing's fish mother had grown enormous, and her beauty had increased accordingly. Xing Xing smiled.

"I want to see her again," said Wei Ping. "You fed her, didn't you? I saw you. I want to feed her too. I think she's lovely too."

"I don't have any food left," said Xing Xing. "And she's gone off. You can feed her the next time you come down to the pool with me."

"I don't want to wait till the next time," said Wei Ping. "I want to see her now." She sat down at the pool's edge. "Come, dear fish," she called. "Come back and let me see you."

But the fish didn't come.

After awhile Xing Xing filled the bucket, and with many rests along the way, the girls returned to the cave.

When Stepmother came in later, Wei Ping couldn't wait to tell her about the fish. "She's huge, Mother. You should see. And she's even prettier than she was before."

"Are you sure this is the same fish?" asked Stepmother.

"Xing Xing feeds her every day," said Wei Ping, nodding. "She feeds her with her *shizhi,* the forefinger she uses to feed herself. Just as though the fish was a family member. The fish comes right up to her and sticks her head out on the bank."

Stepmother looked at Xing Xing so suspiciously, the girl's lips went cold. "I have to see this for myself," she said. She went back out the door.

"Talk to us first," cried out Wei Ping. "Tell us about this mysterious furniture you're having made."

"That can wait," said Stepmother brusquely. She limped down the hill.

It was a long time before she managed to make it back. She dropped onto the *kang,* completely tuckered out.

"Isn't she all that I said?" exclaimed Wei Ping, clasping her hands under her chin. "Isn't she just the most wonderful fish ever?"

"Silly girls make up silly stories," said Stepmother. "But it isn't a laughing matter when it costs me so much toil to go down to the pool and back."

"We didn't make anything up," said Wei Ping. "We're not children. Maybe you frightened the fish.

I must have frightened her too, because she wouldn't come for me, either. But she comes out for Xing Xing. I saw her. And tomorrow I'm going to see her again, and I'll be the one to feed her."

"Is this true, Xing Xing?" asked Stepmother. "Is there really a fish? And does it come out for you?"

Xing Xing was surprised that Stepmother used her real name. Maybe the woman had sensed the presence of Father's spirit. Or maybe she was merely trying to manipulate the girl, like Wei Ping had done this morning. Fingers of dread twined around her throat. She couldn't even swallow the saliva that gathered at the back of her tongue.

But, really, she shouldn't have such a reaction. There was no reason for Stepmother to manipulate Xing Xing. The woman could get anything she wanted from the girl by simply ordering her around.

"Yes," answered Xing Xing, forcing herself to move beyond the unreasonable dread.

"Well, maybe someday you'll show her to me," said Stepmother lightly, as though it were of little importance after all. "In the meantime, if you're still curious . . ." She looked teasingly at Wei Ping. "I have things to tell you."

20 The things Stepmother told them held both girls spellbound. Emperor Hung Wu wanted all of China to be united. As the son of heaven, he was China's leader both morally and politically. He was the one and only person who could mediate between heaven and earth, and he had decided that customs that varied from province to province interfered with the harmonious functioning of the cosmos. Instead, all festivals, from the local to the national, should be similar and follow new ceremonial regulations that would ensure the unity of China.

"Our local cave festival will be very different this year," said Stepmother. "Much more elaborate."

"In what ways?" asked Wei Ping. "Tell us."

"There will be dancing and acrobatics and, well, I don't know everything," said Stepmother. "But one thing is sure: People will come from far away to take part. Men. Who knows, maybe even the local prince will come. He hasn't taken one single wife yet. All the unmarried women are going to dress up beautifully. This is our opportunity, at last."

Wei Ping laughed with the joy of anticipation.

But Xing Xing felt like crying. If all the girls were supposed to dress up beautifully, she couldn't possibly go to the festival, for her clothes were nothing more than tatters.

"And the furniture you're having made?" said Wei Ping. "Tell us about it, Mother. What is it?"

"I'll do better. I'll show you. He assembled it instantly." Stepmother went outside and came back a few moments later saying, "A one-wheeled cart." She pushed it into the room.

Wei Ping scrunched up her nose. "That's a barrow. What will we do with an ugly barrow?"

"You'll sit in it and be pushed to the edge of the festival."

"What? I don't want to arrive in a barrow, like a bunch of radishes."

"No one will see. We'll go through the woods. That's why I wanted the cart to have but a single wheel, which can be easily maneuvered. Xing Xing can grease the wheel with bear fat so that it makes no noise at all. When we get there, we'll stash the cart behind a bush, and you'll come out, as fresh and happy as any girl with bound feet who is carried by a servant."

"That's a good idea, Mother. A very good idea. And will you get Master Tang's slave boy to push the barrow?"

"We don't need him."

"We don't?"

Stepmother looked at Xing Xing.

"Of course," said Wei Ping. "Xing Xing is so strong."

Half of Xing Xing wanted to object. She couldn't face the shame of being in rags when everyone else was in their best finery. The other half of her grasped at any chance to see the dancing and acrobatics Stepmother had talked about. And, after all, shame wasn't called for. Instead, what she should feel is humility. It was good for anyone to feel humility. She met Stepmother's eyes and held them, almost proudly. "I'll scrub my dress and darn the holes," she said.

"No, you won't," said Stepmother. "I'm going in my mourning sackcloth, of course. So you could certainly go in your tatters. But you won't." She went over to her sewing basket and took out the dress she'd finished the night before. "You'll wear this."

"Really?"

"Haven't you worked hard? You deserve it."

Tears of gratitude sprang to Xing Xing's eyes.

"But what about me?" said Wei Ping. "What will I wear?"

"I'll make you something splendid," said Stepmother. "I'll go into the village tomorrow and buy red silk and gold embroidery thread. And I'll make matching slippers for your feet, so they look like perfect lilies."

"Yes," said Wei Ping. "You're full of good ideas today, Mother."

Stepmother tilted her head toward Xing Xing. "Come here."

Xing Xing ran to Stepmother, who held the dress up to her.

"Try it on."

Xing Xing turned her back for modesty's sake. She took off her rags and pulled the new dress on.

"It's large," said Stepmother. "That will allow you to dance better. Decent women should never be in tight dresses."

Xing Xing ran her hands down the front of the dress. The yellow was as beautiful as sunlight. Her fingers touched each claw of the dragon Stepmother had embroidered on the bodice. She was perfectly happy.

"Time to get back to work," said Stepmother.

Xing Xing turned and started to pull the dress off.

Stepmother's hand stopped her. "You have a very different job tonight. Wear your dress and go to the spring behind the temple near the village. Drink deeply of its water and bring a pail of it back to us. But don't hurry. Instead, sit there and compose until dinnertime."

"Compose?" said Xing Xing.

"There will be poetry recitations at the cave festival. Everyone is supposed to compose *ci* verse, with tonal patterns modeled after folk tunes. Master Tang's wife told me you are good at poetry, and surely you know many folk tunes. You can represent our family."

"But what should my poem be about?" asked Xing Xing.

"Unloved wild geese, with broken hearts. Rain cooling the earth. Suffering. You know the sort of thing that goes into these poems. You can do this."

Xing Xing had thought she was perfectly happy just a moment ago, but now she was so much happier. Her breath was as light as a hummingbird's.

21 The spring burbled quietly. Besides the river, there were not many sources of fresh water in this area—the pool near Xing Xing's cave and this spring were notable in a dry land. To one side of the spring was the temple, but in the other three directions spread a well-manicured garden of flowering trees and bushes, with stone statues of monkeys here and there and a pool full of pink lotus blossoms. An artificial stone mountain rose from the center of the pool, covered with thick green moss. Duckweed floated on the surface. Xing Xing dipped her hand in under the tiny leaves; the water below was cool.

A sudden longing closed around her. She wanted to be with Father, to put this cool water on his face as he worked, to dig the clay for his pots, to eat with him and sing with him and rest in the crook of his arm. Her eyes hurt with held-back tears. How foolish of her to feel this way at this very moment. Hadn't

Stepmother just given her a dress more beautiful than any she'd ever hoped to wear? Stepmother had made the dress herself—and she'd chosen Xing Xing to wear it. Her life was changing. The certainty of that should open her to sweetness now, not to sorrow. She should regain the joy she felt as she left the cave to come here. She looked around and willed her eyes to welcome the goodness of this garden.

Her eyes didn't disappoint her. As the sun waned and the air cooled a bit now, too, birds came from their hiding places in the tree canopy and hopped or walked along the water's edge. Black-throated robins and white-throated redstarts. Tiny yellow-streaked warblers and large red-billed starlings. Xing Xing delighted most in the blue-rumped pitta, with its black hood, white collar, yellow belly, and greenish blue back. She sat very still for a long, long time.

The happiness she'd felt at Stepmother's unexpected announcements had made her giddy, and in that giddiness she'd forgotten to bring paper, brush, and ink. That was just as well, though, because a *ci* should be composed with the most attention to its sound rather than to the appearance of the characters on the paper. Indeed, most of the people who would compose *ci* for the cave festival probably didn't know how to write; instead, they'd simply memorize their poems. So, as Xing Xing finally began the poem, she spoke aloud and played with the sounds of words until she was satisfied.

Feathers flutter and brush and slice through the air
Claws scrape and grasp what they dare
Beaks poke and dig and scoop and click
Songs brag and flatter and flick
There's nothing quiet about birds among flowers
Aren't we glad, aren't we lucky, to witness these powers.

Xing Xing got up and drank deeply of the spring, as Stepmother had told her to do. She filled the pail with springwater, as Stepmother had told her to do. Then she walked quickly. Stepmother had told her not to hurry, but she felt she should, because she wasn't going directly back to the cave. Instead, she headed to Master Tang's home. She wanted to try out her *ci* on Mei Zi, to see if her teacher would recognize the folk tune it was based on and to read the reaction in the old woman's expressive face.

But when she got to Master Tang's home, the old man stopped her in the courtyard. "Mei Zi is too busy to be bothered right now," he said gently, after hearing why she'd come. "Show your poem to me." He settled on the bench with a bowl of rice wine in one hand.

"I haven't actually written it down," said Xing Xing. "It's meant to be told aloud."

"Then I'll listen." Master Tang stretched out his legs and leaned back on the bench.

So Xing Xing half spoke, half sang her *ci*.

Master Tang smiled. "Can you run in that fine dress?"

"I think so."

"Then run in a circle for me. Many times."

Xing Xing ran around the courtyard. Finally, she dropped onto the bench beside Master Tang.

"Do you feel better now?" said Master Tang. "You needed a good run."

"I guess I do," said Xing Xing. "But how did you know I needed a run?"

"You must have sat quiet a long time before you composed this poem. Birds among flowers aren't noisy if people are."

Xing Xing laughed.

"You have grown into a very attractive young woman, Xing Xing. That new dress does you justice. Where did you get it?"

"Stepmother made it for me." Xing Xing couldn't keep the pride out of her voice.

"She's generous to all of us these days, it seems," said Master Tang. "Aren't we lucky? Like in your poem."

"Has she been generous to you?" asked Xing Xing in surprise.

"Indeed. That's why Mei Zi has no time to talk with you now. Your stepmother brought us so much food this afternoon, Mei Zi is working with the cook, preparing a meal for all our relatives."

"I'm so glad," said Xing Xing, though a high-pitched hum had started in her eardrums and her stomach felt unsettled. "You've been generous to us so many times, lending us the help of your slave boy."

"It's not just us. Your stepmother had our boy deliver fish to most of the families on this side of the hill." He finished his wine. "Extraordinary, she is."

The hum in Xing Xing's ears turned to a drum that accented every word Master Tang said.

"Come back tomorrow," said the old man. "I'm sure Mei Zi will want to hear your poem. The artistry of it reveals your soul. You are a fine maiden, Xing Xing. As the saying goes, 'When accomplishments and character are equally matched, we then have a person of virtue.'"

Xing Xing bowed her thanks for the kind words, then walked carefully along the path toward the cave, holding the pail of springwater in front of her like an offering. She could smell dinner before she got inside. Delicious fermented soybeans. And other things. Things she knew very well. The drumming in her ears was so loud, she could hardly hear anything else. She entered the cave feeling strangely dissociated from her body, as though she were two people at once: Xing Xing and the spirit of Xing Xing, one walking, the other floating.

She took the new dress off without turning her back to the others. Modesty meant nothing in this moment. She draped the dress across the back of a chair. Her old dress was folded neatly on her bed. She put it on. The hem stuck to her legs. It was wet. She peeled it from her skin and held the hem to her nose. It smelled of nothing new, just all the old familiar things. She pressed it to her cheek, then let it fall.

They ate at the *kang*. Stepmother had prepared a stew of many ingredients, all cut up tiny.

Xing Xing studied the bowl. "Why is everything cut so small?" she asked with a new boldness. Perhaps this was her spirit self, speaking with the voice of a drum.

"*Qie peng*—cutting—is equivalent to cooking," said Stepmother. "And small pieces cook faster and save fuel, so girls like you don't have to gather so much firewood." She picked up her spoon and ate a big bite. Then she yawned. "These days all the best cooks chop food finely, but it's certainly exhausting." She looked over at Xing Xing. "Eat," she said.

"I taste millet and mallow and reeds and bamboo shoots," said Xing Xing slowly, as though talking in a trance.

"And fish, of course," said Wei Ping. "This stew is twice as good as usual, Mother."

22 In the morning Xing Xing squeezed rice and peas into a ball with her hands and nibbled at it before anyone else had woken. She hadn't eaten but a spoonful of the stew the night before, so she was hungry. Still, she saved an extra-large portion of her breakfast and hurried down the hill with the water bucket and carrying pole.

Her beautiful fish mother did not come to the bank.

Xing Xing knew the fish wouldn't come, but at the same time she wouldn't allow it to be true. All night long she had fought off the unspeakable idea. She would keep fighting.

She called out, "Beautiful fish, mother fish, come to me." She walked around the edge of the pool and called and called and called. She called till her throat was hoarse.

Then she got on her knees and searched. She

checked every blade of grass, every stone. No blood. No telltale blood. Indeed, the stones were shiny clean, as though they'd been washed. Every trace washed away.

Xing Xing ran. Over dirt and grass and pebbles and sticks. She ran as fast as she could. When she couldn't run anymore, she threw herself to the ground in an alfalfa field and howled with grief.

The sun burned across the entire sky, and still Xing Xing lay prostrate in the field, as though lifeless. But by the time night came, her ears were doing strange things again. Not drumming anymore. Instead, a voice whispered unintelligible things, like an insistent mosquito, buzzing buzzing buzzing, louder and louder. She sat up and looked around and saw something shaggy leaping away in the distance. Could it be a man? He seemed familiar. Oh, very familiar. The buzzing had stopped.

Xing Xing stood up and brushed herself off. She wouldn't run away. Not yet, at least. She could never bear not knowing for sure.

She had run far; it took a long time to walk home. She woke a doe and two fawns with her steady, thumping feet. A huge spot-bellied eagle owl followed her half the way, and still she didn't stop and hide.

Even when she passed Father's grave, even knowing that she hadn't visited it that day to pay her respects to his spirit, she didn't stop. Father's spirit wouldn't want her to stop. She was almost sure the mysterious voice that whispered in her ear in the alfalfa field was that very spirit, urging her on.

The squeak of the cave door as she opened it woke Stepmother. "Is that you?" the woman called groggily.

Xing Xing went to the foot of Stepmother's bed. She didn't tremble or quake. She was as solid as the ground in the alfalfa field. "My dress was wet when I came back from the temple," she said.

Stepmother raised her head but kept the rest of herself as still as a log. "You must have splashed when you filled the pail."

"Not that dress. My old dress."

"Summer is hot and humid, especially in a cave. Mold grows. Dresses get damp."

"It was wet, not damp. Wet."

"All right," said Stepmother in exasperation. "It was wet. Go to sleep."

"Did you wear it when you went down to the pool?"

"Me wear your tattered dress? What nonsense is this?"

Xing Xing was unstoppable now. "Did you fool the fish into thinking you were me?"

"Hush, child. You'll wake Wei Ping. You'll wake your sister."

"What knife did you use? The cleaver?"

"Have you gone mad?"

"It must have been hard to kill such a large fish, to cut up all that flesh. And then the task of getting rid of it must have exhausted you. You had to carry it all the way to Master Tang's. The whole hillside ate that flesh. Can you hear their lips smacking? Can you hear them?"

Stepmother gasped and went silent. Her head dropped back onto the pillow.

Xing Xing walked to the side of the bed.

Stepmother's hand shot out and grabbed her wrist. "Don't ever say such wicked things in front of my daughter. Ever. Or you'll be sorry you were born."

Xing Xing wanted to shout the whole story. She wanted Wei Ping to wake up and hear it all and scream words of hate at her mother. She wanted Stepmother to lose the love of the person she cared about more than anything else. She wanted Stepmother to feel a loss like the one Xing Xing felt now.

But she wouldn't do that. Not for Stepmother's sake. For Wei Ping's sake.

Xing Xing sank to her knees. Then she curled up on the floor. Stepmother's grip on her wrist finally loosened, and Xing Xing hugged herself into the tightest ball she could make.

In her head she went over the exchange she and Stepmother had just had. She examined every word. There was no clear confession here.

What was the truth?

Stepmother was a smart woman, but Xing Xing would be relentless. If the worst had truly happened, Xing Xing would find the evidence.

23

"Wake up and drink." Stepmother stood over Xing Xing, who was still lying on the floor where she'd fallen asleep. She held out a bowl.

"What . . . ?"

"Don't speak!" barked Stepmother. "Think. Yesterday you disappeared. Then last night you came home raving. You're obviously ill. Don't say any more things that you'll regret. Drink."

Xing Xing smelled the potion and recognized it: wild tea leaves mixed with shallot, ginger, and dogwood. It was known to calm the *qi*—the life forces that make up the spirit.

Nothing could calm Xing Xing's *qi* but the truth. Still, she drank, so that Stepmother might be calmed. And she lowered her eyes demurely.

"That's better," said Stepmother. "Your sister is still asleep. When she wakes, we want her to have a good day, right? We both want that. And we want a good tomorrow. And a good week. You agree, don't you?"

Xing Xing bowed her head.

"Exactly. There will be no more devils to plague us. It's my job to make sure of that. Do you understand?"

Xing Xing bowed her head.

"After the cave festival, after your sister has found a husband, then you and I can talk about your future. I realize you must worry about it. But first thing's first. Your sister comes first. Do you understand?"

Xing Xing bowed her head.

"Then show me you understand. Go about your tasks."

Xing Xing got to her feet and went to do the task Stepmother found most loathsome: emptying the chamber pot. It was important that Stepmother believe she was her old, obedient self. That way, Stepmother would let down her guard and Xing Xing could discover the truth.

"No," said Stepmother quickly. "You're still not totally well. I wouldn't want you to get dizzy and fall into the dung heap. For the next few days I'll do that task. You go fetch the water. Fetch it before Wei Ping wakes."

Xing Xing slowly picked up the water bucket. She slowly picked up the pole.

"Wei Ping will be disappointed when she finds you went to get the water without her. She wanted so much to see the fish. What will you tell her?" Stepmother looked at Xing Xing closely, curious.

"I'll tell her the fish wasn't there," Xing Xing said slowly.

"Yes, that's good. And when she asks where it is, what will you tell her?"

"I'll tell her I don't know," Xing Xing said even more slowly.

"Good. And then stop talking about it. You two spend too much time talking these days." Stepmother was still watching her closely. "All right, then, go. Hurry."

Xing Xing found she couldn't hurry. Her movements were deliberate but slow. She knew Stepmother was still watching her. She saw Stepmother's expression change from curious to satisfied.

Stepmother must have added something else to that potion, something that weighed Xing Xing down.

But it worked only on her body, for her mind jumped from one pinnacle to another on a huge mountain of thought. She watched Stepmother's nose wrinkle as she picked up the chamber pot. The woman was taking over the task she hated most. The woman was afraid Xing Xing might get dizzy and fall into the dung heap. But she wasn't afraid Xing Xing would fall into the pool. It wasn't logical. And what had the woman done with the birdcage that held the raccoon kit? She'd thrown it in the dung heap.

Xing Xing knew what she had to do.

24 Learning is not the accumulation of knowledge, but rather, one thing only: understanding. Father had taught Xing Xing that. To truly learn, you listened first with your ears, then with your heart, then with your *qi*. Father had taught her that, too. Xing Xing understood—her *qi* had helped her understand—that her beautiful fish mother was dead. There was no longer any need for evidence.

What was needed was reverence.

So while Stepmother and Wei Ping napped in the heat of the afternoon, Xing Xing went to the dung heap. She felt no disgust as she sank in both arms up to the elbow. Almost immediately sharp bones jabbed her fingers. She pulled out the long spine of her beautiful fish mother. The ribs still held to it firmly. She carried it down to the pool and washed it thoroughly. Then she separated each bone from the others. She washed them a second time—in her tears.

The pile of bones fit neatly in the scoop of her dress.

Xing Xing carried the bones back home and crawled into the storeroom with the last of Father's pots and bowls. She would keep the bones in the corner. No one else ever entered this room, anyway, so it could become a shrine to her mother. But as she crawled awkwardly across the floor, cradling the bones against her middle, she realized that one of the stones in the floor was loose. Xing Xing dug around the stone with her fingers. When it wouldn't come free, she tried prying with a fish rib.

Under the stone was a hole. In the darkness of the storeroom, Xing Xing couldn't see what was in the hole. But she could feel.

She felt a piece of paper, folded and sealed: a letter. Under it she felt silk and feathers and hard little balls on a string.

Xing Xing moved everything in the hole to one side. She carefully laid in the fish bones. Then she took the letter in her teeth, replaced the stone over the hole, and crawled to the opening of the storeroom. She could hear Stepmother talking to Wei Ping in the main cavern room. So she hid the letter in the bodice of her dress and came out of the storeroom.

"What were you doing in there?" said Stepmother.

Xing Xing looked down at her feet.

"Don't go thinking of selling a pot on your own," said Stepmother. "That would be theft."

"I'd never do that," said Xing Xing.

"It wouldn't take you very far, anyway," said Stepmother. "However much you could carry wouldn't sell for enough coins to make a dowry."

"I don't want a dowry," said Xing Xing.

"Of course not," said Stepmother. She stepped close and whispered in Xing Xing's ear, "I forgot. You already had a husband. You were married to your father."

Xing Xing gasped.

"What did you say to her, Mother?" asked Wei Ping.

Stepmother glared at Xing Xing. "Why did you go into the storeroom?"

"Because I'm sad. The storeroom makes me feel better."

"Are you sad because the fish went away?" asked Wei Ping. "Mother told me you couldn't find her. I am sad about that too. But I'm too big to go crawling around in that storeroom. Besides, it's dark in there. Aren't you afraid?"

Xing Xing shook her head.

"When you're sad, come sit with me on the *kang*," said Wei Ping. "We can play the new game Mother bought me—the chess game. And we can talk and cheer each other up."

"If the storeroom makes Xing Xing feel better, then that's where she should go when she's sad," said Stepmother with a sudden change of heart. "I'll keep you company, Wei Ping. I'm good at games." She nodded at Xing Xing. "Go into the storeroom as often as you like." And with that, Stepmother turned her attention to making the evening meal.

Xing Xing didn't get a chance to look at the letter till she went to the pool to fill the water bucket again. Amazingly, the letter was addressed to her. Her mouth went dry. As far as she knew, the only people who had ever gone in that storeroom during Xing Xing's lifetime were herself and Mother. Father and Stepmother were too big. And when Wei Ping was smaller, she was always afraid of it.

Mother had put that letter there. And now that Xing Xing looked closely at the calligraphy, she knew Father had been the scribe.

She opened it and read:

Dear Xing Xing, My Sparkling One, My Darling,

If you are reading this, then your father has just died, for he promised to tell you of this letter upon his deathbed. Console yourself, dearest: His spirit is joyful now, as it joins me.

Your father wrote this letter for me when I realized I was truly dying. He wrote it so I could talk to you now in this difficult moment.

In this hole are my best things—my cloak and dress and pearls and little things. If you are an adult woman, then the things in this hole are to add to the treasures of your life. If you are still a child, then these things are to be used in whatever way you need. Ornament yourself, if that makes sense. Sell these things, if that makes sense.

My spirit will always be with you.

25 True to her word, Stepmother made Wei Ping a fancy dress. She finished it the evening before the cave festival. When the girl tried it on, her happy face looked almost pretty. "What do you think, Sister?" asked Wei Ping, hobbling back and forth in front of Xing Xing.

Xing Xing smiled. "You will catch everyone's eye," she said. Then she doubled over and moaned.

"What's the matter?" Wei Ping rested her hand on Xing Xing's back. "Are you ill?"

Xing Xing curled on the floor, clasping her knees to her chest. She breathed hard, feigning pain.

"What nonsense is this?" asked Stepmother, standing over her.

Xing Xing didn't answer, and she didn't look up.

"She's in pain," said Wei Ping. "Anyone can see that."

"It's probably just the monthly cramps," said Stepmother. "I'll make a chrysanthemum brew."

Xing Xing stayed on the floor and watched as Stepmother used the bamboo tongs to pick up the rocks they always kept hot in the bottom of the stove. The woman dropped the preheated stones into the cooking pot and added a bit of water.

When the brew was ready, Wei Ping carried it over to Xing Xing. "What bad timing," she said, putting the bowl on the floor beside Xing Xing. "But with luck, you'll feel fine in the morning."

In the morning, however, Xing Xing resumed her deception; she groaned louder than ever. It was quickly decided that she couldn't go to the cave festival after all. Stepmother went to Master Tang's house to borrow the slave boy so that he could deliver Wei Ping in the barrow to the festival. While she was gone, Xing Xing sat on the *kang* and picked lice from Wei Ping's hair and wax from her ears. She groaned regularly.

"Maybe I'll position myself by the fountain," said Wei Ping. "There are benches over there. And a fountain would set off my dress nicely. The red would seem that much redder."

Xing Xing worked pork fat into Wei Ping's hair.

"And I'll smile a lot. I have a good smile. I'll plant my feet on the ground, close together in my new silk slippers, and sit there as still as the Buddha.

Maybe a man with a belly as large as the Buddha's will notice me." Wei Ping giggled.

Xing Xing formed Wei Ping's hair into curlicues that plastered the sides of her face and her neck.

"You're so quiet," said Wei Ping. "You've been quiet all week. And you've spent too much time in that dark storeroom. Talk."

"What is there to say?"

"Ah, you're jealous. Don't act nasty. It's not my fault you can't go to the festival. Write down your *ci,* and I'll memorize it and recite it for you. And I'll take note of everything. I'll describe every last detail to you when we get home tonight."

"Thank you," murmured Xing Xing. She formed a spectacularly fine curlicue on the top of Wei Ping's head. After all, Wei Ping was right—none of this was her fault.

Once Wei Ping was sitting securely in the barrow with her legs folded under her and the three of them—Stepmother, Wei Ping, and the slave boy—had set out, Xing Xing crawled into the storeroom.

She removed the stone from the hole. "Mother, sweet Mother, at last I'll get to see these things you've left me, these wonderful things that touched your body and that I've been caressing in the dark all week." She combed her mother's bones through the tips of her hair. Then she bundled the other contents of the hole together and carried them into the light of the main cavern room.

The luster of Mother's pearls, the fine gold embroidery on her green silk dress, the kingfisher-feathered cloak—all of that stunned Xing Xing. But what Mother hadn't mentioned in the letter was the very thing that drew her the most: a pair of gold shoes. Mother's feet had been bound when she was a very young girl, of course. But even after they were adults, women kept their bound feet covered in beautiful cloths within their shoes. So the shoes were larger than their bare feet, though still quite small.

Xing Xing raced down the hill and plunged into the spring-fed pool and scrubbed herself from head to foot. Then she came back to the cave and slowly, reverently, slipped on the dress and the pearls and the cloak, which practically floated on her shoulders. The feathers tickled her neck, soft ghost fingers. She smoothed her hair and put it up in a bun with the ivory picks she'd found in the hole. Finally, she cradled the gold shoes in her hands.

Shoes were such odd things, really. Feet could do just fine without them under most circumstances. At least, her feet could. So why should her hands tremble so now? Why should her lips part with such fierce need?

Mother had not walked gracefully. No woman with bound feet walked gracefully, no matter how sexy that irregular swing of the hips was thought to look. Yet the shoes seemed to exude grace, as though anyone who wore them could walk through fear, through cruelty, and come out standing strong. Mother was trying to help Xing Xing stand strong by saving these shoes for her. That was it, of course.

If only these perfect shoes would fit.

Her breath suspended, Xing Xing gingerly tried one foot in a shoe. It nestled there like a chick under her mother's wing, not at all strange, though it had been more than a year since she'd worn even loose hemp shoes. She put the other one on and walked softly around the cavern room. Then she went more quickly. Then she danced. With her feathered cloak, she felt ready to take flight. She twirled and laughed, gratitude practically breaking her heart. "Mother, sweet Mother."

She went down the hill toward the park, where the cave festival was taking place. On the way she passed a peony bush that was still in bloom. That was fitting, after all. Xing Xing picked a huge white flower and tucked it over one ear, confident that Mother's spirit was with her.

26 The park had never held so many people at once before. They must have come from every village and town within a few days' distance, at the very least. Xing Xing had worried about how to keep herself from being seen by Wei Ping and Stepmother. Instead, it was easy to get lost in the crowd.

Buddhist monks in brown cassocks walked in weaving lines, beating drums with their palms, fingers, fists, elbows, wrists, knees, even toes. Jewel-bedecked women stood or sat in clusters, their silk dresses heavily embroidered in so many hues, they looked like a fragrance garden. Fans of gold paper with painting on them peeked out from their sleeves. Most of them were thin, and those who weren't did their best to appear fragile nonetheless to the men who wandered around in double-breasted jackets and hats with sashes. A few of those men had long thumbnails, a sign of being part of the leisure class, and most of them were corpulent. They watched Xing Xing walk by, and they instantly perked up. They called out about how pretty she was, dressed in green, a cool, watery dream, feathers fluffing around her neck and shoulders, like a spirit about to take flight. They spoke silly words to call her to them, silly but never clever, never funny. They were dunces.

Xing Xing wouldn't look at those men. She hadn't come to advertise herself for marriage. A girl alone couldn't do that. Young people who married without it being arranged by their parents could even be put to death. In the long week that had just passed, Xing Xing had talked with the spirits of her mother and her father. She had decided that she would marry and leave Stepmother's home; she was healthy and useful—some man would surely want her. But she hadn't yet figured out how to do it without Stepmother's help in the arrangements, for she never wanted Stepmother's help in anything again. A plan would come to her when she was ready. The spirits would help her. Today she was here only to see the spectacles. And what spectacles they were!

She passed a snake charmer and magicians and fortune-tellers. She watched an erotic play by a group of transvestites. She stared at contortionists and acrobats. In a roped-off corner young men played kickball. Nearby, others did archery. There were jugglers and people leaping through hoops and balancing on poles. And everywhere she turned, troupes of musicians kept the air singing with flutes and whistles and bells.

Large oblong tables were set up here and there, decorated with fine cloisonné vases of fresh flowers. Small round trays and carved lacquerware overflowed with precisely arranged foods. Xing Xing used a rice paddle to fill a small bowl with white rice from the huge pot on a table and covered her rice with whatever foods she wanted, just as everyone else was doing. Roast chicken and duck, of course. But also cold strips of sheep tail, which Stepmother called "Mongol food" but which Xing Xing now sampled for the first time. She was delighted to find it delicately tasty. She ate fatty pork and onions and garlic, minced and wrapped in lettuce leaves. With her fingers, she dipped fresh steamed crab into vinegar and ginger. She nibbled on shrimp and venison and rabbit.

A young man who had watched her eating with her fingers offered a set of chopsticks—those sticks for eating that had become so popular. He looked at her suggestively. Instead of blushing, she accepted the chopsticks boldly and walked on, using them to eat noodle and vegetable dishes. She sipped fine wines and munched on lychee, kumquat, loquat, tangerines. She sucked away the sweet flesh of a longan, then rolled the big black seed from the middle around and around on her palm. When men followed her, she paid them no attention, and eventually they gave up and went away, muttering in frustration.

Xing Xing had seen imported foods before. Master Tang and Mei Zi had them on their tables at special occasions, and she'd seen some foreign treats at the market earlier in the summer when she was with Yao Wang. But now she tasted them herself. She put her finger into almost every dish. She ate spinach, cucumber, eggplant spiced with jasmine and cadamom and star anise. She smiled at the bite of black pepper, chili, lemon, coriander, fenugreek, Mediterranean olives. She loved the nuts: almonds, walnuts, pistachios. She reveled in the fruits: figs, bananas, pomegranates, star fruits, coconuts, pomelos.

Hanging in cages at many of the tables were exotic birds. Beside the fruit was a cockatoo with a red beak and green plumage; it must have flown in a jungle far from here. It screamed as people chose their fruit.

Never had Xing Xing wondered much about the

world beyond the thirteen provinces of Ming China. But now she wanted to know if women ever traveled far and wide, if Chinese women ever saw cockatoos flying free. And food—a thing that Xing Xing had hardly paid attention to before—she now found to be a powerful lure. She imagined herself going straight north to the Great Wall on the border of her own Shaan Xi Province, crossing that wall, and heading out into whatever might be beyond. Or going down to the village and getting on a riverboat again, going downriver, down, down, to the Han River and then the wild yellow waters of the Yangzi River, where the winds blew all the time, all the way out to the coast, then boarding a ship to the South China Sea, looking and tasting and smelling and hearing and feeling all that the world had to offer.

The day went too quickly. As the sun waned, men lit lanterns and sat around square tables listening to stories. The storytellers got the attention of the audience by opening and closing fans very quickly and smacking them hard on the side of the table. Some of them beat drums, some strummed lutes. They worked in pairs, using big clappers made of two plates of wood and little clappers made of five pieces of wood. The big clappers began and ended the story and sometimes were used within the story for dramatic effect, while the little clappers kept up a steady background beat throughout the narration. Every story began with the same claim: "If you hear the first part, you'll want to hear the second. If you hear the story today, you'll come back tomorrow for another. If you hear the story tonight, you'll think about it as you sleep." Smack went the fan, and the storyteller whipped out a long red scarf and twirled around once.

Xing Xing stood at a distance and watched. A pair of storytellers caught her attention and held it. In their story one played a teacher and the other played a student. The teacher was trying to get the student to use better language—the imperial language—focusing on mistakes in the use of pronouns: The actors were doing short comedies—*xiang sheng.*

"Say I'm your teacher," said the teacher.

Clack clack clack went the little clappers.

"I'm your teacher," said the student.

Clack clack clack went the little clappers.

"No, no." The teacher shook his hands in the air and jumped up and down. "You're not the teacher. Say it!"

Clack clack clack went the little clappers.

"You're not the teacher."

And on it went, with the audience laughing and laughing. Xing Xing laughed too. When a story was surprising, the men pounded the table with both hands and Xing Xing pressed her hands together.

After awhile Xing Xing wandered over to other tables where men sat settling accounts. She watched as a woman stood behind a man and listened to him negotiate. It took only a few moments to figure out what was going on. The woman was one of his wives, and he sold her. Just like that. She screamed, she pleaded, she threw herself at her husband's feet. But in the end, she had to go stand behind her new husband. Would they have a ceremony, with her face covered by a red cloth? Or was that it—an exchange of person for coins?

How many years had she lived with him? Did she feel tenderly toward him? Did they have children? Were the children all girls?

Xing Xing's cheeks felt heavy. Her eyes closed against the hot wave of questions, as though she would cry. She pressed her fingers to her nostrils to stop her nose from running in this sadness.

A man walked through the crowd loudly announcing the *ci* competition. People gathered to sing their poems aloud. Another man promised to read from a story he was writing that would take pages and pages. It was a new literary form called a "novel." Normally, Xing Xing would have wanted to listen to both. But now, suddenly, she longed to go home. She wanted to get away from men who sold wives and men who bought them.

She opened her eyes and turned, and there was Wei Ping, looking right at her. Stepmother was watching her too.

Xing Xing's heart raced. She ran past them, toward the edge of the park. But somehow she wound up in a stand of Torreya trees. She couldn't remember Torreya trees in this park before, and she'd been here so many times. Branches turned to claws that grabbed and swiped at her. She fell over the roots of a dead tree. When a Torreya decays, it can become a nest for a python. She imagined a snake closing around her middle, squeezing, squeezing. She let out a little shriek and scrambled to her feet and ran, but at random, for she didn't know which way home was; she was lost. That was impossible. An evil spirit must have put a spell on her.

She panicked and changed directions and ran faster. A shoe came off. Alas, one of Mother's gold shoes. She stopped to go back for it. But as she turned she saw a man pick it up. And coming through the trees behind the man she saw Stepmother hobbling as fast as she could.

Perfect shoe. Mother's shoe. Most dreadful loss. Xing Xing ran on, stupefied with grief.

She ran all the way home. She went straight into the storeroom and collapsed in a heap of sobs. When she could finally breathe smoothly enough to talk, she whispered, "I'm sorry." She undressed and folded Mother's lovely things away into the hole. "I'm sorry about the shoe," she crooned, holding herself in her own arms. "I'm sorry, Mother. I'm sorry, I'm sorry."

She crawled out and sat in the main cavern room looking out the overhead window as the very last memories of sunlight faded and stars appeared. She waited for the inevitable screaming of Stepmother, the inevitable cut of the switch, the inevitable banishing from this cave.

But Stepmother and Wei Ping didn't come and didn't come. Xing Xing was too anxious to just stay put. In her old dress she went outside to the jujube trees. The branches should have hung low with the weight of ripe fruit by now. But all the fruit had been picked long ago and given to Yao Wang. The trees looked empty and sad, as though they sensed their unjust loss.

And now Xing Xing remembered the Torreya trees in the park. They'd always been there, she knew that now. Of course. Her fear of Stepmother had disoriented her. Trees were not the enemy; fear was. Fear had made her lose Mother's gift to her. Oh, precious gift—the golden shoe.

Xing Xing wrapped her arms around the trunk of a bare jujube tree. Not a single date. Its thorns stuck out sharply, fending off intruders, protecting fruit that wasn't there. Poor tree. She fell asleep on the ground, hugging the base of the tree.

27 "You wouldn't believe it," said Wei Ping to Xing Xing. "There was a young woman at the cave festival who looked so much like you."

"Not that much," said Stepmother as she popped grapes into her mouth. She had filled her bodice with fruit at the festival, enough to last them a week. "I was only confused because she wore clothes that made me think of a cloak and dress that used to belong to Xing Xing's mother. But those were buried with her, of course, along with all her other fine things. It was simple confusion. The woman at the festival hardly looked like Xing Xing at all; she was quite a beauty."

Wei Ping leaned toward Xing Xing. "Mother thought the girl looked like you so much that she expected to find you dressed in green silk when we got home and missing one shoe. The girl lost a gold shoe."

"We'd drunk wine," said Stepmother. "And it was

late and already getting dark. We couldn't see well."

Wei Ping laughed. "Mother was fuming mad. And then there you were, your old tattered self, sitting in the dirt under the trees, barefoot, like a waif." She went on gaily talking about the festival and everything she'd seen there. And about the men who had told a go-between that they wanted to know more about her.

And that was the end of that. No screaming. No whipping. No banishing.

Xing Xing shouldn't have been surprised. After all, neither Stepmother nor Wei Ping ever looked at her. Not really. A change of clothes, and they didn't even recognize her.

They settled back into a routine of waiting to hear from potential suitors. Each morning Stepmother said that a suitor was sure to come that day with an offer of marriage. And each night she said the next day would bring that offer. By the end of a week, when none had come, her eyes glittered and her voice grew shrill.

Then one morning one of the old women who assisted in marriage arrangements showed up at their door. "The prince is coming," she said.

"The prince?" Stepmother opened the door wide. "Come inside and sit down at the *kang* beside my daughter," she said. "Would you like some tea?"

"Certainly. And what is that pungent sweetness in the air?"

"Figs," said Stepmother. She put one of the remaining figs that she'd saved from the festival onto a tray and offered it to the old woman. "Well, now, I must be having a problem with my ears. I could have sworn I heard you say 'the prince.'"

"You did. He's coming to take a wife."

Stepmother's fingers played along her lips, she was so excited. "What did you say your name was?"

"I'm Xiu Mei. That was a very good fig."

Stepmother got Xiu Mei another fig. "Tell us more, Xiu Mei."

"He's looking for a young woman who was at our own cave festival."

"Really? I was at the cave festival." Wei Ping smoothed her dress and sat up tall. "I didn't think the prince attended."

"He didn't. He heard about this woman from someone who sold him a shoe. Apparently, the woman lost it as she was leaving the festival."

Xing Xing stopped her sweeping. She stood the broom against the wall and listened.

Stepmother gave Xing Xing a sharp glance. "Get on with your work, Lazy One."

Xing Xing took the broom into her hands again, but she didn't sweep.

"Is it a gold shoe?" whispered Wei Ping, asking the question that Xing Xing was sure was on Stepmother's mind as well and that sat on the tip of her own tongue.

The old woman cocked her head at Wei Ping like a curious bird. "How did you guess? It couldn't have been you."

Wei Ping looked taken aback. "And why not?"

"They say she's a rare beauty. The shoe's been sold from rich man to richer man all week long, until it got so expensive only the prince could buy it. As the price went up so did the reports of her beauty. Now she's touted to be the most beautiful woman in the empire."

"Nonsense," said Stepmother.

"So you saw her, then?" asked Xiu Mei. "You admit that your daughter is not that woman?"

"Admit? Why would you use a word like that?" asked Stepmother.

"The prince is going from village to village with the one gold shoe. He's letting every female who attended the cave festival, young and old, try it on. So far it has fit no one. But he will continue looking until it does. And when he finds the one that shoe belongs to, he'll marry her. If you admit your daughter was not that woman, then there's no need for me to put her name on the list of girls to be interviewed."

"I admitted nothing, Xiu Mei," said Stepmother. "I said 'nonsense' because I was surprised that a single shoe could be sold as a thing of value. No other reason."

"Then I take it you want me to add Wei Ping's name to the list?"

"Indeed," said Stepmother. She ran to her money box and came back quickly. She dropped a coin in Xiu Mei's open palm. Then she added a second.

"For your slave girl?" asked Xiu Mei.

"She's not a slave. She's my stepdaughter. And it's not for her."

"Then who?" asked Xiu Mei.

"Me."

28 "How could you?" said Wei Ping. "You're putting yourself in competition with your own daughter."

"Don't be stupid," said Stepmother. "You'll try the shoe first. If it fits you, that will be the end of that. You'll be the wife of the prince. But if it's too small, then it only makes sense for me to try it on. If it fits me, you'll be the daughter of the prince, which is almost as good."

"But you wore your mourning sackcloth to the festival. Anyone who knows you and saw you will remember that. No one would believe you were the girl with the gold shoes."

"If the shoe fits me, everyone will believe it. People believe anything. Look how people believed you composed that *ci*."

Wei Ping flushed and looked quickly at Xing Xing, her eyes full of shame.

Xing Xing didn't care. A stolen poem was a small sham in comparison to everything else. "You promised Father's spirit that you'd never marry again," she said.

Stepmother blanched. Her hands flew up, and she turned in a circle, staring hard into the air. "Have mercy, ancestors," she said in a wheedling voice. "I'd never marry an ordinary man. But this is different. No one would want me to give up such a chance. It's a prince, after all. A prince. I've heard he lives across an arched stone bridge—marble, not the wooden bridges of the countryside—behind vermilion walls, with statues of elephants outside the gates. His palace is measured in units of the ancient *yan* rather than the modern *zhang,* because it's so big. He has legions of eunuchs who wait on him and run the household. When he visits his ancestral tombs, he goes by horseback with a one-hundred-man entourage and returns by barge. It's a level of wealth we can hardly imagine. It would be the best life for Wei Ping." She looked at Xing Xing and blinked fast. "It would be the best life for Xing Xing, too. For all the Wu children."

"I don't think Father ever cared much about riches," said Xing Xing quietly. "He loved simple things. And basic virtues, like loyalty. He expected of us only that we be loyal to him."

"I am loyal," said Stepmother. "Loyal, loyal, loyal. The prince has private gardens, full of flowering plants of all kinds—simple pleasures. The Wu ancestors could have a temple there, designated a shrine. Or, no, it would be better than a shrine—it would be a *citang*—big enough for the whole family."

"It doesn't matter what you call it," said Xing Xing. "They'll know you've been disloyal."

"How dare you talk to me like that! How dare you be so defiant."

"They'll add it to your other offenses," said Xing Xing.

"Offenses! What offenses? Don't talk like that. Misfortunes follow from angry, vengeful ancestors. What I intend is not an offense. How could it be an offense, when I do it for my daughter, for my husband's daughter, for my husband's daughters—both of them?"

"You can keep saying it. You can keep adding me as an afterthought," said Xing Xing. "But they'll know you aren't doing it for me. As will the spirit of my mother."

"The spirit of your mother? What has she to do with any of this? She's not my ancestor."

"But she's mine," said Xing Xing sadly. "Whatever form she took. Whatever form she takes next."

"What do you mean, 'whatever form she took'?" Stepmother's voice was a thin, high screech. "What form did she take?"

"You know as well as I do."

Stepmother's fists pressed against her cheeks. "No."

"What's going on?" asked Wei Ping, frantically pulling on her mother's hands. "What are you two talking about?"

Stepmother sank to her knees, dragging Wei Ping to the floor with her. "It couldn't have been your mother. It was too big. Your mother was small. Maddeningly small."

"You can try to fool yourself, but you can't fool the spirits, and you can't fool me," said Xing Xing. "Never again. You knew the moment Wei Ping told you I fed her with my *shizhi,* the forefinger I use to feed myself. You knew then, deep in your heart you knew, and you fooled me into going to the temple and leaving behind my old dress."

"Feeding who?" wailed Wei Ping. "The fish? Are you talking about the fish? What are you saying?" Tears streamed down her face. "I don't understand anything."

"But you do understand," said Xing Xing. "It's so sad, but we all understand."

29 In the end, Wei Ping sided with her mother. What else could a practical girl do? Xing Xing hardly blamed her. Perhaps if her own mother had done something terrible, she'd have sided with her too. She couldn't know. She'd never been put to the test.

Stepmother made a potion of centipedes, wasps, venomous snake, ants, hair cuttings, menstrual blood, and spit, and sealed it in an urn that she hobbled off with into the woods. She did it all before the girls' eyes—she didn't even try to hide. Xing Xing didn't know what magic the concoction was supposed to effect, but it didn't matter. Mother was beyond Stepmother's powers to harm her now. And Xing Xing was somehow unable to fear for herself. When Stepmother returned with dirt under her fingernails, neither girl said a word.

Xing Xing watched Wei Ping and Stepmother primp themselves for the prince's visit to the village.

Stepmother took off her mourning sackcloth and put on a brocade dress for the first time since Father's death. The two of them painted each other's faces. They arranged each other's hair. Then Xiu Mei came by and announced the most amazing news: The prince was paying private visits to each home. It was the only way to be sure that he tried the shoe on every single girl. Stepmother made Xing Xing clean the cave again. The ormanthus blooms were already open, so Stepmother had Xing Xing scatter the fragrant yellow flowers across the threshold of the cave.

The prince sent gifts ahead of him. By custom, imperial visits were always preceded by gifts. They were beautiful tortoiseshells that made Xing Xing think of the tortoiseshell that Yao Wang used. Stepmother wouldn't let Xing Xing touch them. She got on her knees and quickly gathered up the ormanthus blooms and arranged them in these shells herself, muttering words Xing Xing couldn't make out.

Finally, the prince's retinue came. Horsemen clad in brilliant colors led the way. Soldiers marched into their cave home and knelt on one knee, ready to rise quickly and obey the prince's every command.

Stepmother and Wei Ping didn't know how to behave. They knelt in the most formal way, keeping their bodies erect. Their confusion showed in the stiffness of their shoulders and the way their eyes darted around.

Xing Xing didn't kneel, though. She sat on her bottom in the shadows of the *kang,* her legs tucked under her and her knees spread out in front like a winnowing fan. Children sat that way when they felt lazy. Xing Xing didn't feel lazy. She felt alert and almost angry. This whole thing was a sham, and she had had more than her fill of shams. The prince was supposed to choose a wife by using a shoe. But, surely, many women's feet would fit the shoe. He had to know that. So, really, he was just looking for the woman who pleased him most. It seemed wickedly unkind for the man to make such a show when none of it mattered. Oh, she didn't feel sorry for Stepmother. And given how Wei Ping had turned against her, she didn't feel sorry for her half sister, either. But there were dozens of women waiting to try on the shoe. Hundreds maybe. She felt sorry for them. Innocent women, stupidly waiting.

Xing Xing had changed gradually in the weeks since her fish mother was killed. She was determined to be no one's fool anymore. She felt strong. A strong woman in a world that tried to deny the very existence of such a thing. But she wouldn't be denied. She felt she could leap into fire like the mystics and not burn up.

If she wanted, she could marry this prince. That was true. Amazing truth. All she had to do was produce the other shoe. How odd that circumstances had given her power.

She had no idea whether she would exercise that power. Father used to say that once you understood, truly understood, you would find what you were looking for. That is fate. He said that if there was evil in your heart, you would find demons. Xing Xing's heart held no evil, so she was not afraid of demons. But at this moment she understood only what she was not looking for. So her *qi* lay open, waiting to understand what she was looking for.

And then the prince came in.

His clothing made so much padding around his body that she couldn't be sure, but she thought he was only mildly corpulent. Less than her father. And he was shorter than Father, too. He had a thin mustache, a small wispy beard on his chin, and a longer, pointed slip of a beard on his neck, but he was clearly young—surprisingly young for one who had risen so high in the military. He wore a little red cap with an elephant on the front. Altogether, he seemed pleasant enough, but nothing special. Hardly what one might expect of a prince.

He ordered one of his soldiers to try the shoe on Wei Ping. Only the front half of her foot could get in, of course. He ordered the soldier to try the shoe on Stepmother. But her heel couldn't make it in, no matter how hard she jammed it.

The prince looked crestfallen. "That's it," he said. "You were the last two names on the list. I've tried every woman who went to the cave festival. The shoe fits none of them."

Really? Her mother's shoes were that special? Those beautiful, glowing shoes. Not even Xing Xing had realized their uniqueness, but perhaps the prince had somehow understood that instinctively. Perhaps his hunt wasn't a sham after all. "Most Honorable One," said Xing Xing from the shadows.

"Who's there?" asked the prince.

"It's no one," said Stepmother hastily.

"No one with a voice," said the prince.

"Just my stepdaughter. A foolish girl, given to saying crazy things."

"Did she go to the cave festival?" asked the prince.

"Of course not," said Stepmother.

"Most Honorable One," said Xing Xing, "do you believe her?"

"Shouldn't I?" asked the prince.

"If I were a prince," said Xing Xing, knowing such words were dangerously daring, yet still getting to her feet and coming forward into the light, "I'd want an answer directly from my subject, not via a representative—especially one not chosen by the subject herself." She bowed and got on her knees before him.

"But look at you," he said. "You're far from a prince."

"Justly spoken." She bowed till her nose touched the ground. Then she sat back on her heels again. What next?

The air seemed to swirl around them, through them, faster and faster, almost dizzying her with its chaos, when, in a minute dot of time, everything stopped. Everything became as clear and sharp as a sword point. Her choices boiled down to marrying this prince or wandering far and wide, saying crazy things, becoming the person Stepmother accused her of being. Without a plan and without logic, she leaped into the fire, the freedom and risk rendering her euphoric: "And padded clothing can make one appear fatter and, so, wiser than he is."

The prince jerked his head. "I think you just insulted me."

"Or perhaps I teased you," said Xing Xing. Her breath fluttered like tiny birds, filling the cave, rushing toward their fate. "Did you not just suggest that looks tell the worth of a person, when you clearly don't believe it yourself?"

"The girl is quite mad, I tell you," said Stepmother. "She raves. But my daughter here, she's a fine one."

"I'm talking to the girl—the young woman," said the prince. "Be quiet."

Xing Xing found those words charming. They tapped softly on her heart.

The prince pinched his upper lip between his thumb and index finger in thought.

Xing Xing found that gesture charming as well. She smiled.

The prince looked surprised at her smile. Then delighted. He smiled back. "You're certainly not subservient, whether you make a show of bowing or not." And he laughed. "All right, then. Did you go to the cave festival, Impertinent One?"

Being called impertinent was more charming

still. "Indeed, I did," said Xing Xing. *Tap tap tap* on her heart.

"She couldn't have," said Stepmother. "She was sick."

"I got well quickly," said Xing Xing.

"She doesn't have a green silk dress. The girl with the gold shoes had a green silk dress," said Stepmother.

"And a feather cloak," said Wei Ping.

"Well?" said Xing Xing to the prince.

"Well, indeed," he said back, his thumb and index finger again pinching his upper lip.

She couldn't help but grin.

He grinned back. "Do you have a green silk dress and a feather cloak, Impertinent One?"

"And more," said Xing Xing. "Can you be patient?" She didn't wait for an answer. She crawled into the storeroom and dressed quickly in the dark. Then she crawled out and stood before the prince in the green silk dress with the feather cloak on her shoulders and the pearls around her neck. She held her hands behind her back.

"How on earth?" Stepmother gasped. She and Wei Ping clung to each other in their surprise.

The prince stared, silent. He appeared unable to move at first. Then he blinked, as though he were waking up. "I like your clothes," he said breathlessly.

"And I like yours," said Xing Xing. "Especially your funny hat."

"I'm glad you like it," he said. "It's cotton. I got it in India."

A man who traveled. Oh. Her mind swirled with the air of the cave.

"And now, Impertinent One," he said, with the slightest tremble in his voice, "will you show me whether you are, instead, the truly pertinent one?"

A man who liked puns. Xing Xing's hand responded of its own accord, holding out one gold and sacred shoe. "If you give me that other shoe, I'll have a matching pair," she said.

"Allow me that privilege, please." The prince knelt on one knee and put both shoes on Xing Xing. "You're the one," he said. "You're my wife."

"Is that an offer?" said Xing Xing. "We haven't even exchanged names."

The prince stood. "My last name is Zhu. My first name is Cheng Yun. But I'm called Zhu Zhong—loyal Zhu."

"I like it," breathed Xing Xing. "I am Wu. My first name is Xing Xing."

"Xing Xing," said the prince. "Stars. That's perfect for our dynasty. 'Ming' means 'bright' with a level tone. The word for 'destiny' sounds the same, but with another tone." He moved his arms through the air as he spoke. The sleeves of his jacket crossed before her eyes. "A star is destined to be the brightness of my life. You, dear Xing Xing."

Words of purity. Yet Xing Xing couldn't yield herself quite yet—she couldn't fully trust herself to understand quite yet. "There are dragons on your sleeves," she said softly. "My mother was a carp."

"See?" said Stepmother. "I told you she was mad. Her mother died when she was seven. She's always been a lunatic."

The prince pinched his upper lip. When he finally dropped his hand, his lip was white, he'd pinched so hard.

"Your lip is as white as my mother's scales were."

"Many of us never recognize our ancestors," said the prince at last. "You're lucky. Maybe she has become a dragon."

What a delightful thought. "There are important things about me that you need to know," said Xing Xing.

"Let me hear them."

"I don't want to be bought or sold," said Xing Xing.

"Neither do I."

"I can read and write," said Xing Xing.

"So can I."

"My feet are not bound."

"I noticed," said the prince.

"I have no dowry."

"I need none," said the prince. He stepped closer, and his face grew tender. "Leave this cave now. Leave this woman and her daughter. Come, dearest Xing Xing, come with me. We have the rest of our lives for the rest of your list."

And so Xing Xing put out her hand, with full understanding, and the prince took it.

And the world kept moving, not toward any goal, just going, because that's what life does, as Kong Fu Zi says. And it's bound to be better with a companion who knows how to be tender, a companion you may grow to cherish.

POSTSCRIPT

In the summer of 1997, I taught at Capital Normal University in Beijing, where my modern students wrote modern stories that impressed me with how much the very way they were told was steeped in tradition. And what a wealthy tradition! Whenever I wasn't in class, I was wandering, sometimes in museums, but sometimes just along the road, and sometimes in the countryside to the north, all the way to the Great Wall, looking and listening. When I came back to the United States after that summer, a family friend, Michael Chen, gave me a book on the three perfections. That was the start of an enormous reading list that stretched on for the next six years.

Cinderella stories can be found in many cultures, among the earliest of which are the Chinese versions. While there are multiple and varying Chinese versions, the traditional tales are brief—consisting of a page or two of text—and I have been faithful to details of plot across these various versions. However, the tale here differs from the traditional Chinese tales I have read in three ways: I have chosen to place it in Ming times rather than in Qin and Han times; in a northern province rather than in a southern province; and in an ordinary community rather than in a minority community. These changes allowed me to integrate cultural habits of time, place, and community—notably, the prominence of foot binding and the social revolutions of the first Ming emperor (who certainly was not an entirely positive figure, though his cruelty does not play a role in this book)—that brought the story in a direction that compelled me personally. I offer it with respect and gratitude.